GETTING NOWHERE

A Girl Called Al
Leo the Lioness
The Good-Luck Bogie Hat
The Unmaking of Rabbit
Isabelle the Itch
The Ears of Louis
I Know You, Al
Beat the Turtle Drum
I and Sproggy

GETTING NOWHERE

CONSTANCE C. GREENE

The Viking Press · New York

Copyright © Constance C. Greene, 1977
All rights reserved
First published in 1977 by The Viking Press
625 Madison Avenue, New York, N.Y. 10022
Published simultaneously in Canada by
Penguin Books Canada Limited
Printed in U.S.A.

2 3 4 5 81 80 79

Library of Congress Cataloging in Publication Data
Greene, Constance C   Getting nowhere.
Summary: A fourteen-year-old who feels betrayed by his father's
remarriage and who is the butt of some pranksters'
jokes becomes filled with a hostility that permeates
all his relationships and carries him into a near-tragedy.
[1. Remarriage—Fiction. 2. Parent and child—
Fiction. 3. Family life—Fiction] I. Title.
PZ7.G8287Ge   [Fic]   77-5164
ISBN 0-670-33762-5

TO LINDA ZUCKERMAN

1

IF I EVER GET to kiss Lisa, I'm not closing my eyes. I'm keeping them open for a variety of reasons. One, so I can get a good look at her. Two, so I can duck if she swings at me. Three, I want to see if she likes it. I've had only the one experience with kissing and that wasn't what you might call typical. I wonder what you do with your nose when you kiss a girl. Especially a nose like mine.

I filled the bucket with soap and water and looked under the sink for a sponge.

"Mark, I thought you were going to do your room this morning," Pat said. Her voice was casual, but I could hear the irritation in it and was glad. On a slow day, or sometimes when I wake early and watch the dawn slide under the shade, I think of ways to aggravate Pat.

"I did it already," I said. "Besides, I've got to

wash Dad's car." From where I was crouched on the floor, I could see her sneakers and legs in jeans. Why the devil did she dress as if she was a kid my age? Why the devil didn't she grow up? If there's one thing I can't stand, it's a grown woman pretending to be a teen-ager.

"The vacuum is sitting in the dining room where I left it," she said in a low voice. "Better get cracking before your father gets home. Didn't you wash his car yesterday?" she continued in a conversational tone.

"Why don't you get off my back?" I said softly, just loud enough so I could pretend to be talking to myself if she called me on it. I heard her breathe in sharply, but she didn't say anything. She wasn't ready to do battle yet, that was all. A couple more pushes and she'd come out in the open. It was like guerrilla warfare. A good fight might make me feel better. I had a few things I wanted to say, a few loaded things. They could wait, but not indefinitely.

"Day before yesterday," I said in a tone even I would admit was insolent. "It needs it again. Don't forget it rained yesterday." I brushed past her, careful not to touch her, and went to the garage to wash the car, to smooth and polish it, make it look first-class. Some day, in the not-too-distant future, I'd drive that buggy. Sit behind the wheel, turn the key in the ignition like I'd been doing it all my life, release that brake, and steer it out into the world.

On my way to pick up my date, who would be Lisa, driving through the dark, I'd plan what to say. After I got through the preliminaries, had shaken hands with her father and mother, said, "How do you do, sir?" to make an impression on the old man, patted her punk kid brother on the head, not to mention the dog, I'd escort Lisa down the path, opening the door gallantly, closing it carefully, closing her inside, next to me.

Then what? Well, "Let's drive around for a while," I might say, "maybe hit a hamburger joint. That is, if you like hamburgers." Lisa liked that crack. She laughed, put her hand on my arm, said, "Oh, Mark, you're so funny."

I wouldn't try anything on the first date, no matter what she tried to talk me into. Nothing except a couple of kisses, that is. Just your basic soul kiss. Nothing fancy.

A couple of weeks ago I happened to be hanging out in the kitchen, making one of my justly famous grilled cheese and onion specials. Pat and Dad were sorting out books in the study. I guess they didn't know I was there.

"How's it going with the boys?" I heard my father say.

"Well," Pat said. "Tony and I get along fine. Mark's a different kettle of fish."

I should know by now it's always a mistake to eavesdrop.

"Mark has his guard up." I could hear my father flicking his lighter to get it to stay lit.

"Mark is a tough nut to crack," Pat said. I smiled. You bet your ass he is, lady.

"It's partly his age," Pat went on. "Not entirely, but at fourteen, all your nerve endings hang out just waiting for somebody to stomp on them."

My father laughed, but he didn't sound terribly amused. "Mark's nerve endings have been hanging out ever since he was born," he said.

"Listen, my friend," Pat said, "how about me? What do you think those things sticking out of my ears are?"

My father laughed again and she joined him. This time he sounded young and happy. I should've been glad he sounded that way, but I wasn't.

Someone dropped some books and there was silence. It's gotten to the point where I'm afraid to go into a room for fear I'll find them making out. I'm a growing boy. My sensitivities are easily wounded.

Warm water hit my shoes as I lathered the hood. Oh, you beauty, you're such a beauty. Polish, wax, don't forget the hub caps and the trim. Oh, you're going to be so beautiful.

"At it again, eh?" my kid brother Tony said, parking his bike against the wall. He's only twelve and doesn't mind riding his bike. I didn't when I was twelve, either.

4

"You're going to rub the finish right off that baby if you're not careful."

"You sound just like Dad," I said, polishing harder.

"I do?" I could tell he was pleased. "Guess what, Mark. I'm taking fencing as my after-school activity. Isn't that neat? I get this foil to use and a thick jacket with a mess of padding to protect me from my opponent, and a mask and everything."

He picked up an old broom handle from the corner. "*En garde!*" he shouted, lunging at me.

It hit me in the back. "Knock it off," I told him. "Can't you see I'm busy?"

"What the heck's the matter with you?" Tony asked. Nothing much bothers him. "Where's Pat?"

"Inside, reading dirty books and eating bonbons," I said.

"Hey, she's all right," Tony protested. One of the things that really bugs me is that he likes Pat. "She sure beats Mrs. LeBlanc and all those other tomatoes who passed as housekeepers. And Dad likes her better, that's for sure."

"Tell me," I said sarcastically. "That's what I need is for you to tell me how much Dad likes her. No one would ever guess, the way he's acting."

"Well they're married, aren't they?" Tony tossed over his shoulder as he went inside.

I threw the sponge at his back but it missed.

"What do you know? All you are is a twelve-year-old fink who doesn't know his ass from a hole in the ground." I got behind the wheel, draped my arm casually over the seat and prepared to resume my courtship. It was too late. The seat was empty. I couldn't lure Lisa back.

2

I SHOULD'VE KNOWN. I should've known when Dad first said he had somebody he wanted us to meet. He brought Pat to the house and we sat around talking for a while. Then he asked us to go out to the Stagecoach with them for dinner. He'd never done anything like that with one of his lady friends before. I knew something was up when he asked us later, as if our answer didn't matter, "How'd you like Mrs. Nelson?"

"I thought she was great," Tony said first crack out of the barrel.

"You would," I remember saying in a sour tone. "She laughed at your jokes."

Dad looked at me. "I gather you didn't care much for her. Is that it, Mark?"

"She was all right," I told him. "Nothing special but all right."

Actually, she was pretty. She talked to both of us

7

as if we were people, not kids, which is something you have to watch out for at our age. "Does she have any kids?"

"No," my father said. "She was married for a short while when she was very young. She's been divorced for ten years." That was all. Still, there was something there. I tried not to think about it. Two weeks later Dad told us he and Pat were getting married.

That was almost a year ago.

Right away it was different. It wasn't just that they bought a queen-size bed and got rid of the twin beds in my father's room. Although that was part of it. My father sure spent a lot more time in the bedroom than he had before. But the house felt different, smelled different. My father rushed in every night like a thirsty man straight off the desert.

And she was always there, putting her arms around him, kissing him. They kissed like people in the movies kiss. With abandon. That's the only word I can think of to describe the way they kissed. Tony sat right where he was, grinning. I got up and left, making a lot of noise. Nobody paid any attention to me, but I went on making noise.

Pat was a good cook. Too bad. If she hadn't been, it would've been a point to work on, make a few cracks. But she was. And any time Tony and I wanted to have our friends over, we could. The first time a couple of guys in my class came to see if they could help me fix the clutch on my father's Chevy, I introduced them to Pat simply because she was standing in the kitchen and there was no way out.

"This is my, uh, my stepmother, Pat," I told them. She shook hands with both Ken and Scott, and afterwards they said, "Hey, not bad. She's got a grip on her like a man. She's some tomato."

"If you like old tomatoes," I remember I said. Tony heard me and he wouldn't let go. Tony is very tenacious.

"What's your problem? Would you like it better if Dad had married some twenty-year-old chiquita? Yeah, I bet. I can hear you now if he'd done *that*." Tony will never wind up on a psychiatrist's couch, that's for sure. He gets everything out in the open. He's definitely not a brooder. He lets you know where he stands. Sometimes I'd like to kick him in the teeth, but most times I love him. I wouldn't tell him that, but I do. People like Tony. He's a survivor. He'll survive everything. I won't. I'm a fighter. I get too angry at things. I'm always sore about something. Once when I was sounding off about a kid in back of me who's always leaning over my shoulder asking for an eraser or pencil and I know he's checking my paper to see what answer I got, my father gave me a piece of advice.

"Save your anger for something important, Mark," he said. "Don't waste it on little things. That boy won't come out ahead, cheating. Be angry at injustice and poverty, things that matter, that you may be able to do something about when you're a man."

I've thought about that a lot. Trouble is, I've also tried to stay cool but without much success. If a guy shoves his way ahead of me in a line, I get furious. If someone shoots a basket and makes a point, instead of missing (the way I usually do), it makes my stomach churn. I fight it but I always lose. Sometimes that rage gets its hand around my throat in the morning, and all day long it tightens its grip until by dinner I can hardly breathe. It's stupid but it's there.

The thing that really eats away at me, that nags at my guts so bad it sometimes gives me a stomach-ache, is what I did a couple of months after they got married. It was so dumb, so incredibly stupid I can hardly believe I did it. I must've been crazy. I must've been spaced out of my mind.

I was hitching a ride outside school and a couple of seniors picked me up. I didn't even know them. They dropped me at my house. Pat was on the lawn, destroying dandelions right and left. She had on shorts and a T-shirt.

"Hey, look at that!" the driver, a guy named Sparky, said. "That's all right. That's some piece. I wouldn't mind a little of that. That your sister?"

He didn't say it so she could hear, but I sure could.

I mumbled something that could've been "yes"; on the other hand, it could've been "no." I'm a great little mumbler when I have to be.

"She engaged or anything?" the other guy asked, eyeing Pat.

"Thanks for the ride," I shouted. "See you," and I took off up the walk. Pat sat back on her heels and waved. Those guys in the car looked as if they might put on the brake and come in for the afternoon.

"They gave me a ride," I said, fast. "I don't even know them."

"Oh," she said. I suppose if you didn't know how old she was, you might take Pat for a young girl. She buys all her clothes a size too small, it looks like. I bet she was a cheer leader in high school. If there's one thing that gets me, it's cheer leaders.

"Give us an A, give us a T, give us a blah, blah, blah," and then they break into their routine, swinging their hips, throwing their arms around, leaping in the air. They're ridiculous. You have to have a certain mentality to be a cheer leader, I think.

I went inside and got the milk bottle out and took a long swig. Pat followed me in. "Let me get you a glass," she said.

"I like to drink out of the bottle," I said. I'd been drinking out of the bottle for years before she got here, and I'm damned if I'm going to stop now.

"That's hot work," she said, reaching across me to get a glass of water. She brushed against me. I felt her breast against my arm. I'd never felt a woman's breast before. That's when I did it. I grabbed her and kissed her on the mouth, hard. My nose was smaller then. She stiffened and turned her head away and I almost swallowed her ear.

"What in the name of God are you doing?" she said angrily, rubbing her hand across her face. "Have you lost your mind?"

I turned away. My face felt as if I'd been in the sun for about a day, it was so hot. I said the first thing that came to my mind.

"I suppose you're going to tell Dad," I said.

How's that for a line? How's that for a big-time operator? Kid puts moves on stepmother and then whines because she's going to spill the beans to his old man. Up to then that was the nadir in my life. I've had several nadirs since, but then that was it.

"Listen, Mark." Pat stopped and looked at me. "Mark, if I've done anything to make you think . . ." Again she stopped. I felt as if I'd been turned to stone. If a bomb had exploded in the next room, I still wouldn't have been able to move.

"Let's forget it," she said. "Everyone's entitled to a mistake. That's all it was. A mistake." She walked back outside.

God, I wake up at night still in a sweat, thinking about it. As far as I know, she kept her word and never told Dad or anyone else. If I had any guts, I suppose I'd tell Dad myself. But what for? Talk about masochism. If he knew, he'd be sure I was even more of a degenerate than he suspected.

I had to live with it. It's a terrible thing to be under obligation to someone you hate. Maybe I'd hate her more if she squealed on me. It's hard to say.

3

"**M**Y FEET SMELL," Tony said, taking off his shoes and socks. "They smell fierce," he said with a touch of quiet pride. "I bet they smell worse than any feet in my class."

"Not too many guys are proud of having smelly feet," I told him, kicking at the wastebasket. But I had to give it another shot before it tipped over and spilled out on the floor.

"I wish I was sixteen," I said. "If I was sixteen I could drive and be on my own." I hurled myself into a lumpy armchair I'd bought from the people down the street when they moved.

"That chair always reminds me of pimples," Tony said. "It looks like a whole terrible gross mess of pimples."

I ran my hand over the arm. "It's not so bad," I said. "At least it's mine, nobody else's."

Tony smelled one foot. "Yeah, and you're not

going to have much trouble with guys trying to get it away from you, that's for sure," he said. "You're not even fifteen yet," he added after a pause. "Why not try for the big one five before you press on to the big one six, man?"

"In five months I'll be fifteen. Then it won't be any time at all until I'm sixteen."

"What're you going to do then, join the Marines?"

"Who knows? I might take off a couple years before college. Travel, learn what makes people tick, maybe learn how to sky-dive."

"Pat says her nephew started to sky-dive last year and he's jumped about twenty times already," Tony said.

"If you can believe anything she says," I grunted.

"Pat doesn't lie and you know it," Tony said defensively. "What've you got against her anyway? She's all right."

"I keep hoping she'll go away, like a toothache or the measles."

"I think you're acting crumby about her, if you want to know what I think. You're getting worse instead of better."

"Who asked you?" I said angrily.

"Well, you are, and you know it as well as I do. If you keep it up, Dad's going to blow his stack. You're itching for a bruise. When you're around her, it's like you're made of thorns. Or"—Tony's face lit up—"it's like you're a porcupine and some dog's attacking you, so you let fly with a snootful of quills. If Pat was a dog she'd be full of quills every time you talk to her."

"Who says she's not a dog?" I never missed an opportunity.

"She's nice to us," Tony went on relentlessly. "And what's more, Dad loves her. He's a lot happier now that he's married to Pat."

"We were doing fine without her," I said. "We were doing just fine."

"Speak for yourself." Suddenly Tony asked, "Is it because of Mom? Are you jealous because it's Pat instead of Mom?"

"Don't be an ass." I stood up. "He probably should've gotten married a long time ago, when we were little kids. Right after Mom died. It wouldn't have made so much difference then."

"Who to?" Tony reluctantly put his shoes and socks back on. "Mrs. LeBlanc?"

We both started laughing, rocketing around the room, bouncing off the walls, thinking about Dad married to Mrs. LeBanc. Poor Mrs. LeBanc, handsomely mustached, gone to flesh, as my grandmother says, sporting three large moles on her chin alone. Mrs. LeBlanc had two wigs. When she was feeling fine she wore the red one. When she was feeling down, a black one. To anchor them she pinned a large, distinguished polka-dotted hat on top. One windy day I'll never forget, she was coming up the front path when a gust took both her hat and her wig off over the trees. Underneath, her hair was close-cut and graying, like an aging athlete's, like our soccer coach's, Mr. Whitcomb. She put an ad in the Lost and Found column but nothing ever happened, nobody called. She told us, almost crying, that that hat had cost her a week's salary.

"It was to be my Easter bonnet," she said. We told my father and he gave her an Easter bonus instead of candy.

When we calmed down, Tony said, "What about if Dad and Pat ever have a baby? I think that'd be neat." He held his stomach, it ached so from laughing.

"You're out of your skull," I told him. My voice sounded harsh to my own ears. "They're too old."

"No, they're not. Dad's only forty and she's thirty-six." Tony unwisely plunged on. "Plenty of people have babies when they're that old. My friend Jerry Matthews' mother got married a couple of years ago and now Jerry's got the coolest little sister. I wouldn't mind having a little sister."

Way back, from the depths of my throat, I hawked up a wad of phlegm. I'd been practicing. Expertly, noisily, I shot it onto the mess of papers from the wastebasket, which were still on the rug. It lay there, a glittering gemstone, an oyster without a pearl.

"That'll give you some idea of what I think about

that," I said, pronouncing every word carefully. "Now let me alone. I've got stuff to do."

Tony went to the door. "All I can say about you"—he faced me—"is that you used to be a nice guy and now you're a shit." He closed the door noisily.

I put my head in my hands.

The door opened and I sat up straight, fast.

"And another thing," Tony said in an even voice, "don't ask me for any favors. Not ever again. If it's true that nice guys finish last, you're a sure winner."

This time when he slammed the door, it stayed closed.

After he left, I tried studying. The words rolled off my brain as if it had been coated with lacquer. Nothing penetrated. I went out for a walk, to breathe a little and let some air into my head. I felt clogged and mean. I found two dimes in my pocket. Enough for a candy bar and some change. Enough to take the edge off my appetite.

As I crossed the street, I saw a couple of guys talking to a girl. The tall guy put his arm around the girl and she backed off and started to run. The short one put out his foot and tripped her. The books she was carrying spread out on the sidewalk as she fell.

I ran the rest of the way. "Two against one," I shouted. I was in the mood for a good fight. I hauled off and hit the big guy on the chin. He staggered back. I felt very good. Although I'd done quite a bit of practice fighting with Tony and some of my friends, I'd never actually been in a real fight. I turned back and began to pick up the girl's books. It was Lisa. I couldn't have planned it better. The knight on the white charger wins fair lady. Not bad.

Her hair was wild and so were her eyes. Tears ran down her face. Her knee was bleeding.

"What happened?" I said, handing her the books.

"They asked me for money, the lousy little creeps. I said I didn't have any and they started pushing me around." Lisa screwed up her face and shoved her fists into her eyes and kept on crying. I didn't want to look at her. She was ugly when she cried.

The lousy little creeps attacked me from the rear. That's the way. Always attack from the rear. The little one pinned my arms down and the big one started punching. I kicked back and caught the little one in the shins. He hollered and let go. I started swinging. The big guy aimed a kick at my groin. His feet were enormous and his aim was good. If anyone ever asks what it's like to be kicked in the groin, tell him for me it's everything they say and more. It's agony. I rolled on the ground, holding myself. I couldn't help it. I couldn't get up. I rolled around, sweating and groaning and grunting like a pig.

The two guys took off, and when I managed to

pull myself into a sitting position, I saw Lisa standing there, her hands up at her mouth, staring at me.

"It's all right," I managed to say, "I'll be all right. Go on, get out of here." What I really needed was for her to see me like this. I turned over and retched into the gutter. God, make her go. Make her go, I prayed. A long time later, when I was able to walk, she had gone. I got home somehow and flopped on my bed.

Some knight on some white charger. My insides were so full of rage and pain it was hard to tell which was which.

4

LISA SAID HELLO to me today outside biology class. I was going to pretend I hadn't seen her—to save us both embarrassment. When she said it, she ducked her head and didn't look at me. I think she's shy. After yesterday, why not? Her hair is the color of a horse chestnut. She's pigeon-toed.

The house is filled with the sound of slamming doors. At dinner last night the conversation reminded me of people rehearsing a play.

May I have the gravy? Pass the butter, please. Or: *I saw George Tully today. He asked to be remembered.*

It wasn't a play that would be a huge success.

Tony had seconds on everything. "Great, great!" he kept saying, shoveling it in.

"The coach said we're going to give a fencing exhibition at the end of the year and I'm going to be in it," he told us. "He said I've shown enormous progress. Those were his words, 'enormous progress.' He didn't say that to anyone else, just me."

"Good for you." Pat smiled at him. She smiles at Tony a lot. Almost never at me. "That's marvelous. You'll have to show us your technique. Bring home your foil if they'll let you and give us an exhibition."

I didn't plan it. To say something mean. The words slipped out. "That's like being called 'the most improved player' on the team," I said. "What that means is the rest of the guys are a bunch of klutzes."

In the silence that followed, I could hear myself swallow.

"Mark"—my father dropped the words, one by one, into the quiet—"you might have a more balanced personality if, once in a while, you said something nice, instead of invariably being nasty."

The telephone rang. It sounded unusually loud. "I'll get it!" Tony shouted, pushing back his chair so violently it crashed to the floor.

"It's for you, Mark," he said, coming to the door of the dining room. "I think it's a girl. Either that or it's a guy whose voice is changing," he said, laughing.

"Shut up," I said softly, already half out of the room. "Just you shut up. How would you know the difference anyway?"

"Hello," the voice said. "Is this Mark?"

"Yeah," I answered, cool, like I had telephone calls from girls regularly. "It's me."

"Mark Johnson?" she said. The woods are full of Marks, right?

"Yeah," I said again.

"Well, this is Lisa. Lisa McClean?"

"Oh, yeah," I said. I'm a fast man with the repartee.

"Well, I was wondering. I mean, I'm having a party Saturday night and I was wondering if you could come?"

"I'll have to check. To see if I've got anything on for Saturday," I told her so she wouldn't think I meant my parents.

I held the receiver against my chest so she'd think I was checking. Then I moved it to my stomach. My heart was making so much noise she might hear it.

"Yeah," I said, slow, nice and easy, "that'd be great. What time?"

"Oh," she said. "Time. Well, about seven, I guess."

"O.K.," I said and hung up. I went back into the dining room, whistling.

My father looked at me, amazed.

"That must've been some phone call," he said.

"Who was it?" Tony asked.

"Somebody I know," I said, clearing off the plates.

"No kidding?" Tony's eyes were wide with astonishment. "I thought it was a total stranger." That kid can be an awful wise guy when he sets his mind to it.

"I'm going to a party Saturday night," I said casually. I didn't ask them, I told them and hoped for the best.

"I was going to take us all out for dinner Saturday, to celebrate," my father said. He sounded disappointed.

"Celebrate what?" Tony wanted to know.

"Our anniversary." My father put his arm around Pat. "It's our first anniversary."

"I won't be able to make it," I said. "But you'll probably have a better time, just the three of you, without me anyway."

I swabbed down the kitchen counter, planning Saturday night. My *modus operandi*. I hadn't been to a party with girls in about eight years. Since Cindy Benkiser's sixth birthday party. We threw a few cupcakes around the room, ate the ice cream, broke a couple of balloons, and Judy somebody cried when her mother left her. That was right after my mother died, I remember. Everyone was very nice to me. Mrs. Benkiser, who had been a friend of Mom's, spoke in a very soft tone to me and let me have the booby prize in the potato race which was better than the first prize. I'll always remember that.

I'm thinking of parting my hair in the middle. Maybe that would make my nose look shorter. Or anyway divert attention from it. I have my grandfather's nose, I'm told. All of a sudden it's much too big for my face. If I had the money, I might have a little plastic surgery performed. I read in a magazine about what miracles they can do.

"Thanks for cleaning up," Pat said to me. "You did a good job."

I slapped the dishcloth against the sink. "Yeah, I figured it'd been a long time since the joint was really clean," I said. I swear I didn't plan to shoot her down like that. It just came out. I saw the expression on her face and on my father's face too. He looked angry, very angry.

"Mark," he began in what I recognized was a controlled voice.

Pat put her hand on his arm. "Let it go," she said. "Just let it go. He didn't mean anything."

5

ABOUT A YEAR and a half ago my father and I liked each other. On weekends he and Tony and I did things together. We'd go to the driving range and shoot a bucket of golf balls or go to the zoo or to a hockey game. We'd been perfectly happy, the three of us.

So what if old Mrs. LeBlanc was a lousy housekeeper and a terrible cook? So what if when she was feeling poorly, which was a lot of the time, she nipped at the gin? At least she went home at night.

The thing I remember best about Dad and me and Tony being together was a trip we took to the Danbury Fair pretty soon after my mother died. We took a kid with us who lived down the street. His name was David. When we hit Route 7, the traffic was backed up for miles. Everyone else was going too, it seemed.

The weather was perfect. October's bright blue weather. I can hear Dad saying that. "That's what we get for waiting until the last day, boys. October's bright blue weather brings them out in droves."

"What's a drove?" Tony wanted to know. My father laughed. "A bunch of sheep," he said. We stopped for lunch along the way. David had three bottles of soda. His mother didn't let him have any at home, that's why. He drank them fast, like he thought somebody might take them away. Then he burped a lot. We laughed until "Mr. Johnson," David whispered from the back seat, "stop the car. I'm going to be sick." We pulled over and the kid made it just in time. He barfed all over the rear wheel and looked pale green when he got back in.

"I've got a weak stomach," David said proudly. Then, when we finally found a place to park and went to see the booths of homemade stuff—afghans, jelly, quilts, stuff like that—and the oxen pulling contest, which was our favorite, and smelled the sawdust and the animals and the people, David wanted another bottle of soda.

"I'm thirsty, I'm thirsty," he kept saying. He was a pain.

"Keep your eye out for a drinking fountain," my father said.

"I'm not thirsty for water," David said.

"Too bad," my father said briskly, "that's what you're getting." Then, after we'd dropped David off, and he didn't even say, "Thank you," we went home and had waffles in the kitchen.

"I wish Mom was here," Tony said out of the

blue. He was on his third waffle. "I really wish she was here because she liked waffles a whole lot." He was only four at the time.

"Yes." I can see Dad's face as clear as if it was yesterday. "I wish she was here too." He told us a story and said we could skip our baths. We stayed up a half hour later than usual to watch TV. It had been a very good day. I expect I'll remember that day when I'm very old.

Now, on weekends, Pat and Dad played golf or else they went to antique shops or auctions, looking for bargains. Pat had a collection of enameled boxes and she was hoping to find another one to add to it.

"I wish you'd come with us," she'd said once or twice at first. "You might enjoy it."

Tony had gone. Once. It was boring, he said. "If we brought that stuff home, they'd tell us to toss it out," he'd said.

"I told you it'd be a bummer," I said unsympathetically. "I don't know why Dad lets himself be led around by the nose by that chiquita. He never went to any old antique shops before she came around."

"Oh, he enjoyed it." Tony leaned into the refrigerator to see what was what. "I could tell. He enjoys anything if he does it with Pat."

Yeah, the dark side of my mind sneered, he sure does.

6

I WAS IN MY ROOM, trying to make up my mind if I should call Lisa or not. I wasn't much for using the telephone, but lately I felt more like it. Maybe I ought to call her, just to talk. To ask about the party, who else was going, ask her if she wanted me to bring some of my records. I saw her in school today. She smiled at me. At least I think she smiled. She keeps her head down a lot. Last night, when she telephoned, I realized, was only the second time I had really heard her voice. You can't tell much about a person's voice when almost all they've ever said to you is "hello."

I'd just about gotten up my nerve when I heard the car pull in. Pat had driven Tony to a basketball game at the junior high. I looked out the window and saw her beat-up old car, the body all rusted out, sitting in the driveway. When she married Dad, she brought that car as her dowry. Some dowry. It had more than seventy-five thousand miles on it. My father usually used it to drive to the station. Today he'd taken his Chevy to leave at the garage for an oil change.

I put off the call until I was alone. God knows when that would be. For not having a big family, it seemed as if the joint was teeming with bodies. There was hardly any privacy. Some girls I know have their own telephones. I don't know any guys who do. I can see my father's face if I asked him to let me have my own phone. I can just see it. Forget it.

After a few minutes Pat called up to me, "Supper's ready."

I went down, taking my time. "Where's Dad?" I asked her.

"He's staying late for a dinner meeting."

We were alone in the house. Together. That had never happened before. The two of us.

"I'm not hungry," I said. Which was a lie. I was, very. But I wasn't going to eat with just the two of us staring at each other across the table. I'd do without.

"I want to talk to you, Mark," Pat said. "I'd appreciate a few moments of your time. I have a couple of things I want to say to you." She turned and took something off the stove.

Yeah, babe, I have a few things I want to get off my chest too.

"I'm not asking you to love me," she said suddenly. "I'm not even asking you to like me. I'm simply asking you to cooperate and not make every waking minute a battle between us. You're making your father's and my life hell."

I hooked my thumbs into my pockets. "Man," I said, "I'm into self-preservation. That's all I'm interested in. I figure if I don't watch out for myself nobody else is going to. You and my father, you've got something going. That's your business. I'm into self-preservation, like I said."

It came off exactly the way I'd rehearsed it. I was proud of myself.

Pat put her hands flat on the counter. For a minute she looked at them as if there were words written on her fingernails.

"No," she said slowly, "no, it's not self-preservation you're into. It's self-contemplation. Navel contemplation. You spend so much time looking deep into yourself, trying to figure out why you're not happy, trying to figure out what you're getting out of life when you haven't even begun to put anything in, that you don't have time for anything else."

Her eyes glistened and her cheeks were very red.

"I've tried everything. I'm at the end of my rope. You're doing your level best to make us unhappy and, if it makes you happy, you're succeeding." She ladled something that looked like stew onto a plate and handed it to me.

"Here's your dinner," she said coldly.

"I said I wasn't hungry."

"I took the trouble to fix it, now you bloody well are going to eat it," she said, measuring each word carefully.

"O.K." I shrugged. "If that's the way you want it." I sat down and started in, remembering to chew slowly so I wouldn't look too eager.

We heard a car door slam. My father came in. He was excited. I could tell.

"Put down everything and come with me," he said to Pat. "You too, Mark. I have a surprise. Outside."

Pat blew her nose and took off her apron. "What is it?" she asked.

"It's a present," he said, taking her by the hand. "For you." They went out to the garage. I wanted to see what the surprise was. On the other hand, after what we'd just said to each other, I figured it might be better if I didn't go. Curiosity took over and I followed them.

My father was saying, "It's for our anniversary, darling. I bought it for you."

Pat ran her hand over the shining silver surface of the beautiful little Audi. It had steel-belted radials, front-wheel drive, electric rear-window defoggers, plus dual diagonal brakes and independent front suspension. Plus tinted glass and power steering. The whole garage was filled with the smell of a new car. It was such a beautiful thing I could hardly stand it.

"Oh, oh, oh," she kept saying. "I've never seen anything like it. Are you sure it's for me?"

He took her in his arms and kissed her. I might just as well have taken a huge jump in the lake for all they knew I was there. When they'd finished, he said, "I wanted to get something really special to let you know how much this year has meant to me. And the boys."

She threw her arms around my father and hugged him. I looked at them and right into Pat's face.

"Yes," she said, "you and the boys."

She put her arm through his, and they went back inside the house, leaving me standing there running my hand over the smooth, gorgeous thing. Over and over and over.

7

THE NEXT MORNING I woke up and tried to remember what had happened the night before.
That was special, I mean. The morning after Mom
died I did the same thing. For a second I couldn't
remember she'd died. I knew something terribly
important had happened, but it took a couple of
seconds to ·put it in place. And when something
clicked inside my head and a nasty voice kept saying, "Mom is dead," until I couldn't stand it, I
crawled down to the end of the bed, under the
covers, and didn't come up for air until somebody
opened the door and said my name. Then I wanted
to go back to sleep. I figured maybe if I did and
woke up again, everything would be all right. Mom
would be standing at the side of the bed, smiling at
me, telling me to hurry and get dressed.

Of course, it didn't work that way. I was only
six and didn't know any better.

It was only a new car. That was it. Just a new car. No big deal. I didn't have to go through an elaborate routine to pretend it hadn't happened. All I had to do was go down to the garage and check it out. Now. Before anyone else was awake.

I could hear Tony snoring on the other side of the partition my father had put up to divide the big bedroom between us. That way we had some privacy. Tony wasn't much on privacy, but sometimes when I'd been with people for days at a time, talking, arguing, eating, I thought it was the greatest thing on earth. To be by yourself if you feel like it is a luxury as far as I'm concerned.

I sleep in my underwear. In case of fire, or having the alarm conk out, it's extremely handy. A real timesaver. I hopped out of bed and into my jeans and the shirt I'd worn yesterday and got down the stairs, managing to avoid the two creaky treads. I didn't even stop for food, although I was hungry. Later. Right now not a creature was stirring except me. Dad and Pat wouldn't surface for hours. The joint was all mine.

The entire garage smelled new. There she was, sitting sleek and shiny as a jungle cat. I opened the door and slid into the driver's seat. I slung my right arm along the back of the seat, like a guy who drives so expertly he only needs one hand on the wheel.

"Comfortable?" I turned my head, an enigmatic smile on my face, to look at the beautiful chick sitting next to me. She smiled back.

"You certainly are a terrific driver," she said in a sexy voice. "I feel so safe when I'm with you."

Oh, babe, if you only knew.

A gigantic truck pulled out of a side road, directly into the path of my car. Ahead, little kids trailed off the school bus. With split-second timing, I skillfully maneuvered us out of danger, brakes squealing, spectators aghast.

"That was some job you did of avoiding a collision," a cop said admiringly, motioning me to pull over. "Untold people might've been injured, perhaps even killed, if it hadn't been for your quick action. And you're only a kid!" He scratched his head in bewilderment. "If I was in charge of giving out medals, I'd give you one right now."

Pale and shaken, the girl laid her hand on my arm and said in a trembling voice, "You must be the best driver in the world."

Slowly I let the corners of my mouth lift in a modest smile. "I'm just doing my job," I said quietly.

Fadeout.

"Hey, turkey." My friend Jeff Fields stood unmoving, watching. I don't know how long he'd been standing there. Not too long, I hope.

"You forget today is window day, turkey?"

Two years ago Jeff and I had formed a cleaning service called the J. and M. outfit. He got first billing because his initial came first in the alphabet, that's all. Any household job done better for less. We put handmade cards in people's mailboxes. The response was sensational. I think it was the word "less" that touched the hearts of the populace, because we got more calls than we could handle.

Most folks asked, "Do you do windows?" Neither of us had ever washed a window, so Mrs. Fields gave us a crash course. She stood over us until each pane gleamed.

"In this business," she told us sternly, "it's word of mouth that counts. If you do a good job on your first try, you'll have it made."

She must've been right because, from then on, we did windows until we could hardly stand up straight unless we were on a ladder.

We did other jobs too: cleaned out garages, attics, raked lawns and rebuilt stone walls that'd been torn apart by the winter. I even cleaned an oven for a lady who told me, "If you do a good job, I'll give you a bonus." So I worked my buns off and, believe me, that oven hadn't been cleaned in ten years, and she slipped me a dime. Before that, I'd thought she was pretty. Then I noticed she had no ankles, her legs just sort of slid down to her feet uninterrupted, and her fingernails were dirty. Working for people could sour you for life if you let it. Jeff and I were on our way to our first million. We made up our minds that when we made it we'd be the same sweet, unspoiled kids we'd always been.

"No, I didn't forget." I got out of the car and made for the kitchen.

"Nice boat," Jeff said approvingly. "Don't tell me, let me guess. Your old man gave it to you for passing your math test."

"Naw, he gave it to me because I'm such a good kid." I thrashed around in the cupboard, looking for some cold cereal. I wanted to eat and get out of there before anyone woke up.

"Let's have some eggs," Jeff suggested. He's got a perpetual hole in his stomach.

"No, they'd smell 'em cooking." I threw a couple pieces of bread at him, followed by the jar of peanut butter.

"Whose car is it?" Jeff's voice sounded as if he was at the end of a long tunnel, muffled by massive doses of peanut butter and jelly.

"It's a present," I said. "From my father to Pat for their first anniversary."

"Hoooo-eeee." Jeff whistled through his teeth. "Not bad, not bad at all. He must really dig her."

I threw the dirty knife in the sink and stuffed the rest of the sandwich in my mouth.

"Are you going to sit around on your arse all day or are you getting out into the field of commerce?"

He waved a stiff middle finger at me and we took off.

8

JEFF AND I SPLIT at the corner of Willow and Beach. He had two regular window jobs to the left. I went right. Sometimes, when we're not too busy, we do a job together. But now, with folks crying for our services, we go our separate ways. Mrs. Baumgartner was first on my list. In a way I was sorry. I like to save the best for last. Mrs. Baumgartner looks like an ancient queen or a ruler of men. She's tall and thin and moves with dignity. Her back is very straight and she carries her head as if she was balancing a basket of fruit on it. Mostly she dresses in black: black pants and a sweater or a black dress that reaches almost to the floor. Once I saw her downtown in a black cape that billowed in the wind. People turned to look at her as she passed by.

"Some people wear blue or green to match their eyes," she told me. "I wear black to match mine."

Her gray hair is always neat and tidy. Her face is full of bones.

I've been doing windows and odd jobs for her since the first week we went into business. Her husband, Henry, is an invalid. He seldom goes outside except when it's very warm. Even then she pushes him out to the porch in his wheelchair all bundled up in blankets. Mrs. Baumgartner is all black, Henry is all white—hair and skin. His hands are almost transparent. The fingers on his right hand are stained yellow from smoking.

"I was afraid he'd set the house on fire," she told me, "so I asked him to please stop smoking and he didn't even argue. That was the worst. He didn't put up a fight."

She reads aloud to him a lot. Usually, when I get there, she's reading Charles Dickens or Mark Twain or poetry. She has a voice that makes poetry more interesting than I thought it could ever be.

They were the only people I knew who didn't have a television set. "It's all I can do to face up to the morning paper every day," she said.

Today she met me at the door. "There you are," she said. "I wanted to tell you we won't be needing you from now on." She buttoned and unbuttoned her sweater, fussed with her blouse, settling her clothes down.

"How come?" I asked. "Didn't I do a good job last time?"

"It's not that," she said. "Henry's going to have to go to a home, the doctor says, and I'm afraid we won't be able to afford you." For the first time she looked at me. "You're a good boy and we'll miss you, but that's the way it is."

"As long as I'm here, I might as well do the windows and stuff and you can owe me," I told her. Both my grandmothers live in California, and sometimes I pretend Mrs. Baumgartner is my grandmother. Last Easter she colored an egg for me with my name on it, and for Christmas she knitted me an orange-and-black hat that made me look like a convict, but I wore it anyway. When I went to her house, that is.

A sound came from the living room. It was Henry calling to us, asking us to come see him. Mrs. Baumgartner stretched her mouth into a narrow smile.

"I'm not fooling him, but I keep on trying," she said, and we went to see him.

"It's Mark, darling." She patted his sleeve.

"How are you, sir?" I shouted. I have to control myself when I talk to him. His eyes seem to know me, but it's hard to be sure. She says he can hear perfectly well, but I always shout. Mr. Baumgartner's got hardening of the arteries of the brain. He knows what's going on, it's just that he can't talk and his body's giving out. I wish I'd known him when he was in his prime. He was a newspaper editor and worked all night long and wore a vest every day.

"He was so elegant," she said, "so natty. People don't expect newspapermen to be elegant, but Henry was. He could be stern too, but he was always fair."

Henry's eyes went from her to me and back to her. "Can I get anything for you?" she asked. He shook his head.

"I was just going to have some tomato soup," Mrs. Baumgartner said. "Would you care to join me?" We went into the kitchen. "Oh, he does so enjoy seeing you, Mark," she said. "The way his face lights up when you come does me good. Care for a Saltine?" She passed me a plate of crackers and ladled the soup into bowls. She broke up a handful of Saltines into her soup so that it became a soggy pink mass. I thought it was sort of disgusting, but she attacked it with relish.

"All the time I was growing up, I did this, and if my mother caught me, she made me throw it out and start again with just soup," she said. "Have you ever read Jane Austen, Mark?"

I burned my tongue and shook my head. Jane who?

"Good for you," she said approvingly. "She's one of those people you're supposed to have read. You're not really well educated if you haven't read her, they tell you. And I tell you this. She's a crashing bore. I can't help it. That's the way I feel. My mother read Jane Austen to put herself to sleep. She felt very virtuous reading *Sense and Sensibility*. There are some good things about growing old, and one of them is that you read what you want, and another is you say what you think.

"The eyesight fails, the blood thins, the chin sags, but there are compensations." She got up briskly and rinsed the dishes.

"I better get going," I said. I got the cloths out from the drawer she kept them in and went to the closet to get the bucket and the ammonia.

"Mark," she said, "did you hear what I said when you first came today?"

"I heard you," I said. "I want to do it—wash your windows and rake your leaves. And you're not going to stop me."

I guess you could say we had a Mexican standoff. We stared at each other and I won. She smiled at me.

"Mark, if I had a grandson, I'd want him to be like you," Mrs. Baumgartner said. "And I'm not saying that just because of the windows. I'm saying it because it's true."

"Thanks," I said. Being paid a compliment is pleasant, especially when it's been a long time since you've heard one. Maybe I could move in with the Baumgartners and help take care of Henry so she wouldn't have to send him away to a home. I'd visit my father and Tony on weekends and holidays, and that way we'd be better friends, smile and laugh and talk to each other calmly, in friendly voices. Absence makes the heart grow fonder. Familiarity breeds contempt.

Probably if she'd really been my grandmother, I would've charged her double. That's the kind of guy I am.

9

"**W**HATDYA SAY, TURK, you want to go to the flicks tonight?" Jeff asked me when we were tallying up the day's receipts.

"Can't," I said. "I'm going to a party."

He put his hand on his stomach, half closed his eyes and swayed like a willow tree in a hurricane. "Is this here party a stag affair or are there going to be members of the opposite sex there?"

"It's just a party," I said. "All you can eat and drink. Maybe we'll play spin the bottle a couple of times. Turn off the lights and make out. Have an orgy. How do I know? I'll let you know tomorrow."

"Where's this party taking place? Maybe I'll hop on my Honda and whiz by, and if I like what I see, I might stay for a couple of beers." I figure Jeff and I qualify as the original Walter Mitty kids, always phantasizing. I'm going to ask Mrs. Baumgartner if she ever reads Walter Mitty to Henry. I bet he'd get a kick out of it.

"It's at Lisa's house. Lisa McClean's house." I liked the feel of her name on my mouth.

Jeff frowned. "She that girl turkey with the knobby knees sits in front of you in biology class? How come she didn't ask me?"

How'd he know if her knees were knobby? "Yeah, that's Lisa," I said stiffly. I told him about rescuing her from the two creeps. "Jesum crow!" he whistled, rolling his eyes. "No wonder she invites you and not me. You're a hero!

"If that old Lisa knew what a peachy dancer and all-around lover I am, she would've asked me," Jeff said. "On the other hand, I don't think I'm ready for a boy-girl relationship just yet."

Jeff was better-looking than me. He was cool, easygoing. He had two brothers, both older, and two sisters, younger, and his mother and father hollered at them and at each other a lot. I liked going to their house. If Mrs. Fields hollered at Jeff for something he'd done, she included me. She hollered at everyone. It made me feel, I don't know, sort of cozy when she let go at both of us.

"You can come if you want," I told Jeff. "Lisa wouldn't mind."

He shook his head. "This flick is about a guy who gets frozen in an iceberg for two thousand years. All of a sudden there's this gigantic thaw and when he comes up for air there's this gorgeous blond chiquita, practically naked, see, giving him mouth-to-mouth resuscitation."

"I think I already saw it," I said. "See you around," and I cut out for home.

Tony was reading comic books on my bed when I got there.

"Why don't you ever read anything good, for Pete's sake?" I said.

"Hello there, Scrooge," he said slowly. "How are things down at the orphanage?" For a kid who reads so many comic books, Tony does all right.

"Read on your own bed and quit messing up mine," I told him. I wanted to get to work on trying my hair parted in the middle, and I didn't feel like having a twelve-year-old brother as an audience. I had a bottle of hair tonic stashed away in my bottom drawer. I knew if Tony saw me using hair tonic, he'd give me a hard time.

Slowly he got up and dragged toward the door.

"Tonight's the party, huh?"

"What? Oh, yeah, I guess. Now scram."

"When you feel up to a duel, let me know," Tony said. "Swords or pistols."

"Don't tempt me, baby," I said. I had a new comb just for the occasion. Usually I use my fingers. They do a pretty good job. Tonight was different. Tonight was my big opportunity. For what, I wasn't sure. Tonight or never. I could feel it in my bones.

10

A MIDDLE PART was like an arrow pointing to my nose, saying, "NOSE," in big red letters. I gave up and settled for my old hairdo, which was sort of your basic Cro-Magnon man. My blue shirt was clean, and my khakis. I brushed my teeth, sprayed the old pits, and made sure my socks matched. I was so adorable Lisa would swoon when she caught sight of me.

I went downstairs. My father and Pat were in the living room having a drink. Tony was sitting with them, laughing and talking like he was a master of ceremonies or something. He wasn't on the sauce yet, so he was drinking a ginger and ginger. Jeff and I had tried a shot of his father's bourbon once when we were alone at his house. Either we made the drinks too weak or too strong. Whatever, they tasted lousy.

"There he is," my father said. He sounded

pleased. That's one nice thing about him, he always acts glad to see me. Or he used to. This was a big night for him. He felt good, I could tell. "Come and join us. Have you had any dinner or does this party include dinner?"

"I left some meat loaf in the oven if you want it," Pat said. I hadn't talked to her since last night. Or looked at her either, for that matter. From the corner of my eye, I could see she had on a blue dress.

"I'm not hungry," I said. "Thanks anyway." I added that to make my father happy. It was his anniversary, wasn't it?

"What time is your party?" my father asked me. He and Pat were holding hands.

"Seven," I said. I'd checked the time just before I came down. I checked it again. Only six-thirty-five. "I better get going," I said.

"We'll drop you off," he said cheerfully. "Our reservation is for seven and it's a bit of a drive."

That's what I really needed. Even in a car like that new one, to be dropped off at a girl's house. At my age. "It's only two blocks. I can walk."

"How about getting home? You want us to pick you up?"

"Dad," I said, "I'm a big boy. I can walk home." Holy jumping catfish.

He laughed. "All right. You've got your key if you get home before we do. We'd better get going. Have a good time, Mark."

"You too," I said.

They went out, the three of them, Tony on one side of Pat, my father on the other, I watched from the window. They beeped the horn as they pulled away. For a minute I wished I was with them. Then I remembered where I was going. For once I could look at myself in the mirror without worrying about somebody catching me. Maybe in five years, with a nutritious diet, six more inches, and a course in body building, I'd be a smash. Girls would knock down walls to get at me. Until then I'd have to muddle through on my wit and personality.

Six-forty. I turned on the Saturday night news. Nothing new. A couple of bombings, an airplane hijack, a report on what was happening to the price of coffee and wheat and a few more jollies. If I walked slowly, I wouldn't be early. I didn't want to look too eager.

I'd been past Lisa's house lots of times, hoping to catch her in the yard so we could have a spontaneous conversation. I never had. I stood under a streetlight and checked my watch. Still five minutes to go. I walked around the block one more time, dragging my feet, taking my time. There was no moon. Too bad. I understand moonlight makes girls feel passionate. The second time I arrived at Lisa's house, I figured this was it. I went up the walk, onto the porch, and knocked on the front door. I listened to the sounds coming from inside—the TV and a dog barking. No one answered so I knocked again, harder. The porch light came on and the door opened.

"Hello," I said.

The man looked at me over the top of his glasses. "Yes?" he said.

"I'm here for the party," I said. "My name's Mark Johnson." Why is it I always feel like such a fool when I say my own name?

"I don't know about any party," he said.

"Lisa invited me. I'm in her biology class." I felt like saying, "Didn't she tell you I saved her life the other day?" but I didn't. We stood looking at each other. Sweat ran down the insides of my arms. Something rustled in the bushes around the porch. The dog barked in the back of the house.

"Lisa!" the man hollered. "What's this about a party?" He didn't ask me to come inside. I stood there under the light until Lisa came into the hall.

"This young man says you invited him to a party here tonight," the man said.

"Hi, Lisa."

"Oh, hi," she said from her hiding place behind her father.

"What's this all about?" he said sternly. "Did you invite him, Lisa?"

"No, Daddy, I'm not having a party," Lisa said.

"Ohho." Lisa's father smiled for the first time. "I thought so. You youngsters will try anything these days, won't you?" I thought he was going to slap me on the back, he seemed so jovial all of a sudden.

"Ohhohoho." It was a sound he made deep in his throat, not a laugh, just a sound. "Guess you've got the wrong house, eh?"

I stood there like a statue, looking at Lisa, and her father looking at me.

"It must've been somebody else," I mumbled. "It must've been somebody else named Lisa. I know quite a few girls named Lisa." I backed off. "Well. Good-bye."

I turned and went down the steps, forcing myself not to run. They stood and watched me go. I could hear somebody laughing in the bushes. There was a lot of scuffling. I saw two guys, one tall, one short, running away. A small voice told me they were the same two I'd rescued Lisa from. They were hollering and laughing so hard I heard them for days after. In my sleep even, I heard them. If I'd had a gun and could've caught them, I think I would've killed them.

I started walking. I walked a long way. I went past Jeff's house and saw some lights on in the kitchen. Maybe Mrs. Fields was home and I could talk to her. It was Saturday night. She wouldn't be home on Saturday night. I walked some more. It started to rain. I put my face up to the rain and it got in my eyes.

When I got home, it was seven thirty-five. I could hardly believe that was all it was. It felt like four o'clock in the morning. I took the meat loaf out of the oven and ate from the pan. Then I went to my father's liquor cabinet, got out a bottle of Scotch and poured out two fingers, straight. I drank it down in one shot, the way they do in Westerns. My eyes watered again. I must have fat fingers. One way or the other, either the rain or the booze wound up in my eyes. I went to the bathroom and threw up in the toilet.

The house felt cold. Empty houses get cold faster than houses with people in them. I put on a sweater. It still felt cold, so I wrapped a blanket around myself. There were mostly reruns on TV so I knew when to laugh. I ate some pretzels, considered having a beer and decided my stomach wasn't up to it. At the stroke of ten, sort of like Cinderella, I turned off the set and went to bed. Just in time. I heard them come in downstairs, laughing and talking.

"I guess Mark's already home," I heard my father say. Pat said, "I hope the party was a success," then I heard Tony say something, probably a wisecrack. They sat around and talked for a bit, then the sound of doors opening and closing. Tony came upstairs and looked at me. I lay on my stomach and breathed deeply and regularly. As soon as he hit the pad he started to snore. I think he needs to have his adenoids out.

I lay there listening to the sounds of silence.

When they began to deafen me and the pounding in my ears shut out even the silence, I got up and very carefully went downstairs. Through the darkness, which I knew well, I went to the kitchen and out to the garage. She was there, filling every corner; so grand, so sweet smelling, so new. I circled her without touching. With a piece of old sheet, I polished her hood, the trim, the headlights.

I like to tell myself that nothing was planned.

Tony's fencing foil lay in the corner. He'd brought it home over the weekend to practice. The teacher said he could. I picked it up and held it the way I'd seen him do.

En garde. Thrust. Lunge.

The tip hit the driver's side of the silver-gray car. Barely moving, I dragged the foil along the unblemished surface, leaving a delicate, almost invisible line.

But it was there. I knew it was there. Like a wound, a scar. It would never be perfect again.

After it was done, I put the foil back in its place, went back upstairs, and lay looking at the ceiling until I heard the birds begin.

11

"**A**ND I HAD a slice of roast beef this thick!" Tony held his fingers apart to show me. "And Yorkshire pudding, and I went to the salad bar three times and nobody stopped me. And you should've seen the dessert tray." His eyes grew round and he stopped talking for the first time in fifteen minutes while he thought about the dessert tray.

"There was lemon meringue pie and chocolate eclairs and strawberry shortcake and a bowl of whipped cream to put on everything that was so deep you could've drowned in it if you wanted. And the waiter let me have two desserts."

"How was your party?" Pat asked from where she stood at the stove frying eggs.

"O.K.," I said. "Where's Dad?"

"Bob Evans picked him up to play golf."

I opened the door to the garage. The car was

there, breathing. "I've got to do a few jobs I didn't have time for yesterday," I told them.

"On Sunday?" Pat raised her eyebrows. "At least have something to eat."

"I'm not hungry. I'll be back in a few hours." Time enough for what was coming. When I woke up I felt as if I'd been running all night long. Running and getting nowhere. I had a headache.

In this dream I had, the guys hiding in the bushes tied me up and kept kicking me in the groin until Lisa's father came out on the porch and said, "Stop that racket." She was hiding behind him, smiling, pointing at me. When I woke up, my pajamas were so wet I thought I was bleeding. I checked. There was no blood.

I walked on for a while. I kept my head down and was careful not to step on any cracks in the sidewalk. To me stepping on a crack is like walking under a ladder. Bad luck.

All along I think I knew I was going to see Mrs. Baumgartner. She was the only person in the world I could bear talking to right now.

She came to the door in her bathrobe, frowning. "Not now, Mark," she said in a cross voice. "Henry had a bad night. I didn't get much sleep and, to make it worse, my son's coming today."

"Oh," I said. I turned away and the tears came to my eyes. I felt as if she'd kicked me too. As if my last friend in the world had said, "Get lost."

"Why don't you come back in a couple of hours," she said in a softer tone. "That way I'll get a chance for a rest and maybe Joe won't stay long. It depends on whether he has a golf game or not."

"O.K.," I said. If I'd had enough money, I would've gone to the movies to kill time. As it was, I walked around town, up and down streets I'd never seen before, looked in a few store windows, then sat down on a bench in the park and watched a couple of little kids fight over a bicycle.

"How come you kids are fighting?" I said, to get a conversation going.

They stopped hitting each other. "We just like to," one said.

She'd said to come back in a couple of hours. I made myself wait two hours and forty minutes. Try that some time. When I finally allowed myself to turn into the Baumgartners' street, I walked very slowly, passed the house once, then turned around and came back. Talk about self-control.

"Did your son come?" I said when she invited me in.

"He called and said he couldn't make it," Mrs. Baumgartner said. "He said he'd come next week. Joe doesn't come often because he doesn't like to see his father the way he is now." She sounded bitter. "It embarrasses him. He doesn't understand that Henry is the same gentle, good man he was before. Henry has a loving heart. If you know someone with a loving heart, Mark, consider your-self lucky."

"I don't have one," I said. "I hate a lot of people."

"Listen"—Mrs. Baumgartner pointed her finger at me—"don't tell me about hating. I know all about hating. It's loving I had to learn about. I'm still learning. You look surprised." She turned her back to me. "I'm a very impatient person. Before Henry's illness I lacked patience. But, as I said, I'm learning."

"I did something terrible last night," I said and told her what I'd done to the car.

She turned to face me. "There's one thing I'm sure of, Mark. And that's that you and only you are responsible for the kind of man you become. I found that out a long time ago. It may be the only thing I'm sure of. Don't make excuses for your-self."

"Suppose I don't want to become a man," I said. "Suppose I decide to be a kid for the rest of my life. Do what I want and never mind anyone else. Sup-pose that's what I decide."

"You look as if you're ready for a fight," she said. I realized my fists were clenched. "I suppose you had what you thought was a good reason for doing what you did to the car. But about staying a child all your life. If that's your decision, I feel sorry for you." Mrs. Baumgartner went to the window and looked out. "But I'm even sorrier for whoever moves through your life. Your wife, your parents, your children."

So I told her about the phony party and how I went to Lisa's and how Lisa's father cut me up into little pieces and fed me to the guys in the bushes. I didn't tell her about the fight and what they did to me because I didn't want to have to say "groin" to her. I thought maybe she was too old to hear that word.

"Poor Mark," she said. "Now you'll have to face your father and he'll be furious."

"Maybe he won't know I did it," I said. "Maybe he'll think it was scratched in a parking lot. That happens lots of times. A guy parks too close and opens his door and nails you."

She shook her head. "Remember one thing. It takes a lot of energy just to stay alive, to go on living. It doesn't matter whether you're your age or mine. Energy is what you need. And hope. In the long run it's worth the effort."

I said good-bye and walked around for a while longer. Then I headed for home.

12

THE MINUTE I WALKED IN, I knew that my father knew.

"Hello," I said. I opened the refrigerator and pulled out an apple to give my hands something to do. He sat at the table looking at me. Pat got up and started to peel some potatoes. I could hear Tony's radio upstairs.

"Mark," my father said, "I want to give you the benefit of the doubt. I want to think you're not responsible for the gash on Pat's new car. That it happened last night at the restaurant and whoever did it didn't have the guts to let me know himself. Tell me that's the way it was."

It took all my strength to look him in the eye. The trouble was I didn't have enough energy left to open my mouth and tell him how it'd been, about last night, about what was going on inside me. Not that that was an excuse for what I'd done. I knew it wasn't. It just might help him to understand.

He started to pace back and forth. I saw Pat give him an agonized look. That's the right word, the word I want. She looked at him and her eyes were full of agony. Not for me. For him. Sometimes it seemed as if everything was for him. If I ever do grow up to be a man and have kids of my own, I'll spread it around. People are supposed to remember what it's like to be a kid.

"Will you say something in your own defense or will you let me assume that you deliberately, with malice aforethought, marred that car simply out of bad feeling toward Pat and me?" my father asked me. He waited. I opened my mouth.

"Yeah, I did it," I said. Even to my own ears I sounded smart ass. I didn't mean to; that's the way it came out. "I won't lie to you. It was me."

It was the only way I could get to you. I didn't say that, I thought it. I wasn't going to defend myself.

"But it wasn't malice aforethought. I didn't plan it, it just happened."

Pat wiped her hands carefully on her apron and left the room. It was just as well. This was none of her business anyway.

"It's not so much the car, although, God knows, that's bad enough. It's the feeling behind it. What's happened to you to make you have so much hate in you?" My father put his hands behind his back, probably so he wouldn't put them around my throat.

"I'll pay to have it fixed," I told him.

"And that'll make everything all right—is that what you're trying to tell me?" My father's voice got louder.

"Maybe I ought to run away, go live some place else, come and visit on Sunday once in a while." My voice trembled.

"That's not such a bad idea," he told me. "Don't go wallowing in a sea of self-pity, either. The way you've been acting around here for the past few months indicates there's a lot wrong."

My father put his hands in his pockets. He was getting closer. "A lot wrong. I realize you dislike your stepmother, for what reason God only knows. She's done everything she could to be pleasant. She's a good person and she's willing to try. But we can't go battering our heads against a stone wall forever. That's what it's like with you, battering against a wall."

Something rose from the pit of my stomach and hit the back of my throat. It tasted yellow and vile. It crawled up to behind my teeth. If I kept them tightly closed, whatever it was might stay there and not come gushing onto the floor, maybe even hit my father in the face.

"I'll tell you what's wrong," I started to shout. "I'm your son. All you care about is her, hopping into the sack with *her*. Pat this, Pat that. There's not enough to go around, Dad. You don't know squat about me, what I think, who I am. I'll tell you who I am. I'm your son!"

The kitchen was very quiet. The house was listening. From a long distance away I saw my father's face, the contempt on it, the anger, the rage. Almost with relief, I saw him raise his hand. It had been a long time coming.

He hit me against the side of my head. Hard, very hard. It rocked me back.

"Yes," he said slowly, doling out the words as if they were hot and bitter, "that's true. You are my son. And, believe it or not, that's something of which I was once proud."

He left me then, alone. The sound of breathing filled the room. It was me. I drank a glass of water. I wasn't going to get sick. I wasn't even going to cry.

The telephone rang and I answered.

"Hey, turkey, how was the orgy last night?" Jeff asked.

"As orgies go it was all right," I said.

"Is that all you have to say?" He was indignant. "You been running?"

"What?" I said.

"You sound like you been running the mile in nothing flat."

"No," I said. "It's been kind of rough around here, that's all." I felt the side of my face where my father had belted me. "I'll see you around."

"The only guy I know who goes to an orgy and doesn't get all the facts," Jeff said. "If it'd been me, I would've taken a camera."

13

BREAKFAST WAS GRIM. My father pretended I wasn't there. Tony sat looking at all of us as if we were insane. Pat put four spoonfuls of sugar in her coffee, then didn't drink it.

Rain was pelting down like a son of a gun, which spoiled my plans for playing hooky. Usually Tony and I walk to school. The junior and senior high schools are separated by the athletic field. I could pretend I was going inside, then slip away and he'd never know the difference. The rain finished that plan. Pat insisted on driving us. Anyway, I'd had so much trouble in the past few days I didn't have the strength to cope with a day in a deluge. Besides, what would I do? Huddle under an awning, get my feet wet, and wind up with pneumonia. It wasn't worth it.

Biology was the first class of the day. Lisa was in her seat when I got there. She also pretended not to see me. Today was obviously not my day. She was bent over so far it looked as if she'd dug a hole in the top of her desk and planted her head in it.

All right. That's O.K. If that was her father's way of doing things, she couldn't help it. Could she? She could've at least said something to me besides, "Oh, hi," as if I were some kind of an awful creep who frequently molests girls and goes to parties that aren't. She could've at least said something to her old man that might've made things better. But no. All I got was an "Oh, hi." Who needs it?

When the period was over and Mr. Adamson had given out the assignment for the week, the way he does, I waited until everybody had left. I figured if I played my cards right, the guys who'd pulled such a lousy trick on me would tip their hands and I'd hit 'em in the jugular. There was some way to get even and I was going to find it.

Lisa was waiting for me at the door.

"Mark," she said, head down, "about the other night. I told my father—"

"Listen," I said, "your old man must've been a big wheel in Hitler's SS troops. I can see him now, pounding on the doors at three a.m., dragging the little kids to the gas chambers. He must've got his kicks from things like that."

My ears were red. I could feel them firing up. Her ears got red too. Her hair was shorter than mine and I could see them. At least she finally looked at me.

"You don't have to be so mean," she said fiercely. "How'd he know who you were?"

"Because I told him, see? But he's your father. You have to live with him. I feel sorry for you, toots," I said and took off.

"Slow down, buster," a guy on hall patrol said. "I'll slap a demerit on you if you keep on running like that." I already had seven demerits for misbehavior in the halls. Ten and I'd get suspended. Big deal. If they suspended me, I'd take off like a rocket. I'd pack a lunch and build myself a raft and go down the Mississippi. Look around for Tom Sawyer, Huckleberry Finn, one of those guys. They really knew how to live.

The day dragged like a turtle out for a walk. A fat, old turtle. It was exhausting, always being on guard. In the cafeteria at lunch, I kept watching guys' faces, wondering if the kid sitting across from me or down at the end was the one.

"What'd you do Saturday night?" my friend Ken asked me.

"What's it to you?" I snarled.

He almost dropped his sandwich and backed off. "Wow, what's eating you?" he said. "You got a toothache or something? I only asked because I called you up to come over on account of my father made us a pizza, from scratch with his own hands, and I figured you might want to get in on it. It was the best pizza I ever ate. Anyway, I called up your house and nobody answered so I figured you had to be somewhere else."

"Sorry," I mumbled. "It was my father's anniversary. We went out for dinner." That was a white lie. A lie but one that doesn't hurt anyone. If you have to lie, it's the only kind.

By the time the bell rang at three o'clock, I was ready for the booby hatch and the loony bin, rolled into one. I decided I couldn't keep it up, looking for the bad guys. I'm not naturally a suspicious person. Which is a good thing. It takes too much out of you.

"Take my books home for me?" Tony came to my locker. "I've got fencing practice. Tell Pat I'll be late."

I fooled around for a while, cleaned out my locker, shot a couple of baskets, killed time like it was a mortal enemy. I didn't know where to go. I didn't want to go home and face Pat. On the other hand if I went to see Mrs. Baumgartner, she'd begin to think I was a pest.

Then I remembered it was Monday. Pat took piano lessons over in White Plains on Monday. She was learning to play jazz piano. A middle-aged woman shouldn't play jazz. If she's going to play at all she should stick to the classics.

The house was empty again. I seem to spend a lot of time in an empty house. Maybe somebody was trying to tell me something. I ate a can of spaghetti so I wouldn't be too hungry for dinner. Maybe they'd think I was sick. My father might start to worry about me. Who was I kidding? If I fell down on the floor and my face turned blue and my eyes bugged out, he'd say calmly, "That's perfectly normal for a fourteen-year-old hoodlum. Don't disturb yourself. Just let him lie there and he'll be all right in three or four days."

The air in the empty garage was heavy with new car smell. All of a sudden I slammed my hand into the wall. It hurt something fierce. Talk about being a glutton for punishment. I slammed it again. The pain in my hand made the rage inside me seem a little less.

I went upstairs, turned the radio on full blast, put the pillow over my head. My hand throbbed. I got up and took an aspirin, then went back and crawled under the pillow again. After a while I thought I heard the telephone ringing. Let it go. I turned down the radio. Sure enough.

I ran down the hall and stubbed my toe on a chair. I cursed a lot and picked up the receiver. It was dead.

I just got back under my security pillow when the phone rang again.

Let it, I told myself. I nearly broke my leg getting to it this time.

"Hello," I shouted.

I could hear breathing on the other end. "Hello," a voice said. "Is this Mark? Mark Johnson?"

I closed my eyes to clear my head of the blackness that filled it. When I opened them, the voice said sweetly, "Is this Mark baby? I'm having . . . a . . . party . . ." and then the giggling began. There must've been four of them at least. They were busting their guts laughing. I hung up quietly so they wouldn't know I'd hung up. Then I took the receiver and threw it against the wall. It bounced and landed on the floor where it lay, humming at me, endlessly, filling the whole house with its sound.

14

WHEN I GOT to Jeff's house next day I could hear his mother yelling at him.

"I don't care who's coming over, you're not going anywhere until you pick up those records. All, not half. All." She came to the door and let me in.

"Mark Johnson," She caught my name on the tip of her tongue and tossed it in the air. "Get in there and help Jeff clean up that mess. I don't care if you helped make it or not. There are plenty of times you *have* helped and then skinned out scot free."

"Old turkey," Jeff muttered as we went to work.

"I'd like to see you call her that to her face," I said.

The blood drained out of his face and he put up his arm to ward off an imaginary blow.

"Hey, you want me to wind up mince meat? You want me to get myself beat up by a dame? My

mother is some strong bimbo. And you know what?"
He sat back on his heels. "She's starting to take a
karate course at the Y next week. Everyone around
here is walking softly, I can tell you. My father,
my brothers and sisters, even Amy." Amy was the
baby. She was ten and almost as big as Tony. She
got away with murder. "I bet if they ran a Powerful Mom contest, she'd win hands down."

Mrs. Fields put her head in to observe our progress. "You missed one. Under that chair. And
when you finish, there are some brownies in the
kitchen. Mark, I met your stepmother in the store
last week. She's a lovely woman. You're lucky your
father married such a nice person." She sat down
on the bed and watched us work. "If there's one
thing that gladdens my heart," she said, "it's seeing
young folks working their fingers to the bone. She
said she and your father play golf. Maybe we could
play together sometime."

"Yeah," I said.

"Mom," Jeff's sister Amy hollered, "I can't find
my catcher's mitt. I need it right now. Have you
seen it?"

"It's either under your bed or in the refrigerator," Mrs. Fields yelled back. "Wherever you left
it.

"And she's lucky to get such a nice pair of step-
sons." Nothing ever stopped Mrs. Fields from
completing a thought once she'd begun. "I told

---

her I thought you were a fine boy. Your father did a good job of raising you boys. Now it's nice he's got someone to help him," she said, peering at me.

Amy saved the day. She bounced in, brandishing her mitt. "You'll never guess where it was! Under my pillow. I hid it there last night. We have quite a few light-fingered people in this house. Hi, Mark. I'll be home for supper, Mom. 'Bye."

Mrs. Fields stood up and looked at herself in the mirror. "I look older than I did yesterday and younger than I will tomorrow," she said. "Catch me next week and you'll hardly recognize me. *Ciao*."

"What's 'chow' mean?" I asked.

"It's Italian for 'so long,'" Jeff said. "My mother's taking a crash course in Italian so she can go to Rome and see the Pope."

"I didn't know she was Catholic," I said.

Jeff shrugged. "She's not," he said.

We ate some brownies and drank some milk. "Has your father ever hit you?" I asked Jeff. "When he was really angry."

"Plenty of times. Once I put a book inside my pants when I'd done something—I can't remember what—and when his hand came down on that book, you should've heard him yell," Jeff said with a great deal of satisfaction in his voice. "Boy, didn't he holler!"

"I don't mean hitting on your rear end. I mean, you know, sort of on the face," I said.

Jeff thought for a minute. "I guess not. Not on the face. Just on the padded areas. My mother hit my brother Bart with Amy's baseball bat last year. She caught him on the fly. He said something really fresh to her and then ran up the stairs. She caught him halfway, laid that old bat across his behind and broke it. Amy cried and Bart ate his dinner standing up. Want another?"

"No thanks," I said. "My father hit me on Sunday."

"Yeah? What'd you do?"

"I gave him some lip about Pat. That and I sort of messed up the car."

Jeff's eyes were round. "The new car?" he said in a whisper.

"Yeah. I scratched it. It's going to cost a lot to have it fixed. I said I'd pay."

"How'd you scratch it?"

I told him. He said, "Man! You don't mess around, do you? That's pretty heavy, Mark."

"I don't need you to tell me that," I said. I opened my mouth to tell him about the non-party at Lisa's, then shut it. The time wasn't right. Maybe it never would be.

We fooled around a little bit with Jeff's brother's new headset. It was cool. When I put that set on and listened to the music, the rest of the world was shut out. I couldn't hear anything but beautiful sound. If I could just walk around with a headset on for the rest of my life I'd be in business.

"I've gotta go," I said at six.

"See you."

Mrs. Fields waved to me from upstairs. She opened the bedroom window.

"*Arrivederci!*" she hollered. "*Arrivederci, Marco!*"

I waved back. I figure when Mrs. Fields hits Rome, it and the Pope will never be the same.

15

MY FATHER BROUGHT home an estimate for fixing the damage. He handed it to me without comment. $173.84. That was a lot of windows.

"I'll get another estimate from the body shop on the Post Road tomorrow morning," he said, "but I don't expect it'll vary much."

He headed toward his study. "I've got some work to do, Pat," he said. "Don't hold dinner for me," and he went in and shut the door.

"Mark, what's bothering you?" Pat asked me.

"Me?" I looked around to make sure who she meant. "Nothing's bothering me."

"I'd like to talk to you," she said. "Please sit down."

"I can talk standing up," I said.

"That's part of it."

"What's part of what?"

"What you just said. You can talk standing up. Every time I make a move, you pull back. You put up your guard. Why do you dislike me so much?"

"I don't dislike you," I said, spacing each word carefully, laying emphasis on "dislike."

She put her hands in her pockets. " 'Dislike' is perhaps not a strong enough word for what you feel toward me." Her voice trembled. "That's what you meant, wasn't it?"

The tomato was sharper than I thought.

"You father is miserable about the other day. He won't tell me what happened, what you said that made him hit you. I know it was something insulting to do with me. He's too kind, too much of a gentleman to tell me, even if, by telling, I might understand better. He feels terrible about having hit you. He said, 'I never thought I'd do such a thing to a child of mine. What's happened to me?' "

She crossed her arms in front of her. "If you don't care about what you're doing to me, surely you must care about him." She waited for me to say something.

I got myself a glass of water and drank it slowly. When I'd finished, I said, "Don't worry about it. I'll only be around a couple more years. Then you can have him to yourself."

"I'll give you credit, Mark," she said. Surprised, I made the mistake of looking at her. Her eyes were filled with tears. "You're playing it very smart."

"I am?"

"Yes," she said. "You know if you cause enough conflict around here, if you make things sufficiently unpleasant, our marriage will suffer. It can't help suffering. And that's what you're really aiming for."

She ripped off a piece of paper toweling and blew her nose. "There's one consolation. If it all blows up in my face, at least I'll know I tried. I tried my damnedest but I can't fight forever."

She left the room and me, standing there.

Last year Mrs. Fields told Jeff and me about the son of some people she knew who had killed himself. He didn't get into his father's college, although his marks were very good. His father had counted on it, had told all his friends his son was going to his alma mater. He let the kid know how disappointed he'd be if the kid didn't make it. So when he got the letter telling him "sorry," he went up into the attic and hanged himself. Mrs. Fields said there must've been other reasons, but I'm not so sure. The kid pasted his letter of rejection on his mirror where they found it, after.

I can see Mrs. Fields's face when she said, "Imagine having that on your conscience. As if it mattered what college he went to. How awful to be them, that mother and father. They'll have to live with that for the rest of their lives."

I considered knocking myself off. My father would have to live with that for the rest of his life. I could tape up the estimate from the body shop on my mirror for him to find. That'd make him feel pretty bad.

On the other hand, it might make me feel pretty bad too. If I was dead, I mean. That's what is known as cutting off your nose to spite your face. I had to take that into consideration. There were quite a few things I wanted to do before I kicked the bucket.

What was it Mrs. Baumgartner had said? It takes a lot of energy just to stay alive, she'd said.

Maybe she has something there.

16

"I'M GOING TO POSE a hypothetical question," Jeff said, gumming his twenty-five-cent cigar like a Hollywood mogul. "If you had a date with a gorgeous bimbo, sensationally gorgeous, and everything goes like clockwork, you use the right fork, the R-rated movie is pretty good, the car doesn't break down, you pull up in front of her house, her mother and father are out drinking and her granny is asleep with her hearing aid on the table, what do you do?"

Tony lay on the floor picking his toenails, transfixed. His beady little eyes traveled back and forth between Jeff and me, waiting.

"I'd ask her what good books she'd read lately," I said. "How do I know what I'd do? You been wetting down that cigar for weeks now. Why don't you light a match to it, smoke it, something? It's disgusting."

The end of the cigar Jeff put in his mouth most often was beginning to fray pretty badly. He'd Scotch-taped the worst of it, but it hadn't done much good.

"Don't avoid the issue," Jeff said. "You wouldn't know what to do, right?"

"Depends whether it was the first date or the second," I said, stalling. "What would you do?"

"I'd put my hand on her knee and tell her I respected her, if it was my first date," he said.

"What about if it was the second?" Tony asked.

"Hey, hey," Jeff chortled, thumbs in the air, "that's a different story. First, you have to make her trust you. Let it slip that you're an Eagle Scout, never forget Mother's Day, help old ladies across the street. Use a potent after-shave and brush your teeth after every meal."

"And if all that fails, you can always hit her over the head and, when she comes to, tell her most girls you take out are similarly affected by your charm," I said. I didn't like talking about sex with Tony around. He was too young. Let him wait a couple of years.

"Did you make out with girls at that party you went to Saturday?" Tony asked.

I flicked a wet towel at his bare legs, hitting him just right.

"Hey!" He sat up, rubbing the spot, glaring at me. "What 'd you go and do that for? That hurt."

"It was supposed to," I said.

Why did I want to hurt him? He was a good kid. He was my brother and he'd done nothing to me.

"What makes you so sore at the world?" he wanted to know. "Why are you so angry all the time?"

"I'm not," I said in a surly tone.

"Yes, you are. Everything I say, you snarl at me. You're getting to be a pain in the butt."

He clattered down the stairs. Jeff stowed his slightly used cigar in his pocket.

"The kid has a point," he said, not looking at me. "I've got to split. My old lady threatens extermination if I don't get home early tonight. See you," and he was gone too.

I've got a voice inside my head, screaming at me.

Before he got married, my father had a talk with me. "No one will ever take your mother's place, Mark," he told me. "Pat knows that. It's important that you do too."

"That's O.K., Dad," I remember saying, anxious to get this over with. "If you want to get married, go ahead." I gave him my permission. I didn't know then what a difference it would make.

"Just one thing more I want to say," my father went on. "Remember, it takes time and patience and effort to love. And to make love. Loving isn't necessarily easy or even always pleasant. A person you love can hurt you more than someone you don't care about. Because of that some people are afraid of committing themselves, are afraid of getting

involved, so they never love anyone but themselves."

For a brief minute, I remember, he put his hand
on my head. It felt light and warm, resting there.
We very rarely touched each other. Sometimes, on
the television news or in foreign movies, I've seen
men embracing one another, hugging, kissing.
Maybe they're fathers and sons, maybe brothers,
maybe just friends. I think that's a European cus-
tom. Nobody thinks the guys are sissies, nobody
accuses them of being queer. I think it's kind of
nice.

In a way, my anger lets me get around the room.
Without it, I might not move.

The voice inside me tells me to do hurtful things,
makes me do things like whipping the towel against
Tony's legs. Up until about a year ago I never
heard it. Now it lived inside me, never left me.
Sometimes it was so loud I couldn't hear anything
else. It shut out the sounds of love. It was taking
over.

17

WHEN IT HAPPENED, it was like a ripe plum falling into my lap. I was in the principal's office waiting to see Mrs. Murray about my English test.

"You going to call him tonight?" a voice I recognized came from out in the hall. Something turned over in my chest. It might've been my heart except that it was too big to be a heart. I inched closer to the door to hear better.

"Why not?" The snicker was familiar. "We got him on the ropes, let's polish him off. He's got it coming. What say we invite him to another party given by some other young lovely next Saturday? That ought to pin him against the wall."

It was them. The same two. The rear attackers, the groin kickers. Rage made me strong. They were facing each other. I put up both my hands, one on the back of either head and shoved as hard as I could. I moved like greased lightning. They didn't know what hit them. Their skulls came together with a satisfying clunk. A hollow sound. I hoped it felt like running into a stone wall in the middle of the night. From the expression on their faces, maybe it did.

"It's lucky for you," I told them, "that I don't have my twenty-two with me." I was pleased to note that my voice was calm and even. It was only my bones that were trembling, deep inside me, where they couldn't see.

"If I did, I'd shoot you both. I'd aim for the gut. That's what pros do." They looked at me as if I were crazy. And, in a way, I was.

"Stomach wounds are nearly always fatal," I told them. I'd read that somewhere last week.

I walked back into the office and caught Mrs. Murray coming out. For once in my life the timing was perfect. It was like a well-executed play in baseball or basketball. Everyone did what they had been practicing. There were no slip-ups.

When I came back into the hall, it was deserted.

For the rest of the day I was filled with a sense of exhilaration. It was a terrific, unaccustomed feeling that I wouldn't have minded getting used to. I smiled at everybody. I held the door open for someone's mother and gave her directions on how to get where she wanted to go.

"Why, thank you," she said in a surprised voice.

"You're very kind." I could almost hear her that night at supper, telling her husband and her kids that at least *some* young people still had manners, giving her children the hairy eyeball the whole time.

If I'd been a businessman, today would be my day for making a stupendous deal. A multimillion-dollar deal. If I really was going to take up sky-diving, this would be the time to start. Nothing could go wrong with me today. It was my time to howl. I'd hop out of that old airplane, skim over the tops of trees and rivers and lakes, and make a perfect three-point landing.

Today I was invincible.

I had planned to stop after school at the Baumgartners' to check on what needed doing. First I stopped at the Hartleys' to collect what they owed me.

"Come back tomorrow!" Mrs. Hartley shouted. She was dyeing her hair at the kitchen sink. This week she was going to be a redhead, I could see.

Mr. Baumgartner was sitting in his chair, his eyes not so dim, a little color in his cheeks. He looked pleased to see me.

"Doesn't he look beautiful?" Mrs. Baumgartner stood back, her head to one side, admiring her husband. "I've always loved that tie. You look so handsome." She kissed him. He raised his hand off his lap slightly. I know if he could've, he would've touched her.

"Is there anything you want me to do?" I asked.

"Has something nice happened to you, Mark?" she said, studying me. "You look happy. You should smile more often. Smiling becomes you. I'm glad to see you look happy."

"I am," I said. I don't think she would've liked to hear what made me happy, so I didn't tell her. A car pulled up outside and the doctor came up the steps, carrying his black bag.

"I'll check around outside and see what stuff I have to do," I told Mrs. Baumgartner as she showed the doctor into Henry's room.

I checked the garage and the yard and got out the clippers and went to work on the hedge that screened the garbage pails. Even to me, the place was starting to look run-down. Especially compared to the other places around. It took a lot of work to keep a joint in shape, that's for sure. There were a couple of panes of glass that needed replacing and the house could stand a coat of paint. On the trim, anyway. And I had to get to work earning the money to pay my father back. Still, if I got myself organized, I could manage my other jobs and have a few hours a week free to work here.

The doctor and Mrs. Baumgartner came out onto the front steps.

"You're running yourself into the ground," I heard him say.

"No, no," she protested.

"If anything happens to you, I'd never forgive myself for not doing something, for letting you go on this way. I'm afraid it's time, Martha." He put his hand on her shoulder, and she stared at her feet, not saying anything.

"I'll make the arrangements," the doctor said slowly. "I'll call you within a few days and let you know."

He got into his car. Mrs. Baumgartner went back into the house. After a couple of minutes, I followed her. When I called her name, she didn't answer. I walked to the bedroom door and tapped. There was no sound so I looked in. They were sitting there together. She had pulled up a chair and was patting his hand gently, over and over, while Henry smiled into space as if something wonderful had just happened.

18

"**S**OMETHING SMELLS GOOD," I told Pat. She looked over her shoulder. When she saw who it was, she stopped what she was doing.

"It does?" she said.

My sense of exhilaration, of power, was so strong it had lasted even through what had happened at the Baumgartners'.

"Yeah," I said magnanimously. "What is it?"

"Stew," she answered. She looked at me and I smiled at her. Tentatively she smiled back.

"Your father and I are going to have dinner and go to a movie tonight," she said. "I fixed dinner for you and Tony. Just put any leftovers in the refrigerator, will you?"

"Sure," I said.

She kept looking at me as if she wasn't exactly sure who I was.

A face appeared at the window over the sink.

"Hey, Mrs. Johnson," Jeff called, "can Mark come out to play?"

Pat started to laugh. She laughed harder and harder until tears were streaming down her cheeks.

"I don't know why that's so funny," she said, gasping for breath. "Jeff, would you like to stay for supper with the boys?"

In a flash the face disappeared and Jeff was sitting at the table in an attitude of anticipation.

"I'd be pleased and honored to stay," he said. "That is, if my mother will let me. My mother blows hot and cold. Sometimes she's glad there's one less mouth to feed. Other times she acts like I suggested that she and my father go to a nudist camp for the weekend. Her voice gets all uptight and scratchy and I can practically see her pursing her mouth."

"Do you want me to call her?" Pat suggested.

"That'd be great," Jeff said. "Have a sort of heart-to-heart with her, will you? I mean, ease into the subject gently, then when she's softened up, let her have it. A lot depends on what we're having for dinner at home. Whether she's got plenty of grub or whether she's scraping the bottom of the barrel. If there's not enough to go around, she'll be glad to get rid of me. On the other hand . . ."

Pat had already started to dial. "How are you?" she said to Jeff's mother. "I was wondering if Jeff could stay for supper with Mark and Tony. We're going to the movies. . . . Yes, I'll tell him. See you soon, I hope."

Pat hung up. "Your mother says fine as long as you're home by eight to do your homework. There's ice cream in the freezer."

She went upstairs to change. Jeff and I hung out in front of the TV set to catch the evening news. Something about kids watching the news that lulls parents into a sense of security. They figure if the kid cares about what goes on, if he displays an interest in world events, he can't be all bad. It's the other programs, with the good stuff like murder and drug pushing, maybe a little singing and dancing thrown in, that gets them all tensed up.

My father came home, washed his hands, said a few polite words. Then he and Pat jumped into the silver chariot and peeled off.

When they were out of sight, the three of us sprawled at the kitchen table like a bunch of philosophical cowboys in a saloon.

"You have to look at it this way," Jeff said, brandishing his cigar. "If nobody ever told you about sex, you might not want to try it. Right?"

Tony makes himself small when he's sitting around and the conversation turns to sex. He's afraid we might leave something out. What he doesn't know is how little we really know. We just know more than he does.

"Same with smoking pot or drinking booze or eating clams on the half shell," I said. "If you hadn't read or heard about them, you wouldn't have any curiosity either. On the other hand, that doesn't make you a better person. My theory is, in order to be well rounded, you've gotta throw yourself open to experience, live life to the fullest."

"Hear, hear," Jeff said. "My point exactly. Don't hold back. Let yourself be buffeted by life's storms."

The glazed look left Tony's eyes. "One minute you guys are talking about sex, the next it's clams," he said in a complaining voice. "I wish you'd pick a subject and stick to it."

"The kid is understandably confused," Jeff said. I ladled the stew onto plates, put some bread and butter out, and poured us each a glass of milk. We ate with our elbows on the table, swooping the bread around in great arcs to get up the last of the gravy. We polished off the ice cream. Each of us had three scoops with chocolate sauce.

"A delicious repast," Jeff said, heaving a sigh of contentment. "My compliments to the chef."

"I've got an idea," I said. "Let's go for a spin to top off the evening." I felt so good I didn't want the feeling to end.

Tony looked at me as if I'd lost my marbles. Jeff said, "Spin? Whatdya mean, spin? You haven't got wheels."

"Oh, yes, I do," I said. I took the key to Pat's old buggy from the hook on the wall.

"How about if we hop in and take her around the block once?"

Tony's eyes were huge and round. "You're kidding," he said. "You wouldn't dare."

"Don't come if you don't want," I said. "I can't help it if you're chicken."

I put the plates in the sink and tossed the empty ice cream cartons in the trash. "Jeff, how about you?"

"What if a cop decides to stop you and ask to see your license?" Jeff asked me. "What'd you do then?"

"I'm not planning to go on the throughway or the parkway or any big deal like that," I said. "Just around the block." If I couldn't sky-dive or negotiate a million-dollar deal, the least I could do was drive around the block in a beat-up old car.

Jeff studied the end of his cigar. "It's against my principles to say no to a friend," he finally said. "Let's go."

We went to the garage and climbed into the car. At the last minute Tony came too. "I don't think this is such a hot idea," he grumbled. "What would Dad say?"

"Nobody's forcing you," I said. "Nobody's twisting your arm." He huddled in the back seat, scrunching down so his head barely cleared the windowsill. We both knew what Dad would say.

I'll say one thing for that car. It started right up. It was old and ugly and nobody in their right mind would bother to steal it, even if the keys were left in the ignition, but it started right up. One turn of the key and the engine purred, ready to leap into action.

I put her into reverse and backed out of the garage. I'd done that plenty of times. Actually, I backed up less jerkily than I went forward.

"You know what you're doing?" Jeff said.

"Does the Statue of Liberty stand in the harbor?" I shouted, easing her into first until we hit the street.

"Fasten seat belts!" Jeff hollered. That car had come off the assembly line long before seat belts were invented. I turned to the right, gained momentum, and threw her into second. She jerked and coughed and stalled out. I was in fourth instead of second.

"Sorry," I said, starting up the powerful engine once more. First, second, third. We were actually driving down the street. I concentrated on keeping away from the curb, not too far over on the left. Air whistled through the windows, the trees seemed to bend in the wind. I felt as if I were flying. Charles Lindbergh must've felt like this when he hopped into the *Spirit of St. Louis* and started across the Atlantic. I had never felt so good, so powerful, in all my life. Not even this morning. This was a day to remember.

I checked the speedometer. We were doing fifteen miles per hour. I pressed my foot on the accelerator and hit twenty, twenty-five. The street was deserted. On either side, lighted windows showed people eating dinner, TV sets glowing like great blue eyes. Think of what all those peasants inside were missing.

"Hey, slow down," Tony said from the back seat.

"Relax. Big Brother is in charge," I told him. At the end of the street I brought her to a smooth stop, put her into neutral, then first, and eased her around the corner and into second. I shifted so smoothly their heads didn't even wobble.

"Smooth as a baby's behind," I sang out.

Why not cruise past Lisa's house? She lived only two blocks away. With any luck at all, her father might be out on the curb. I could whip my wheels up on the sidewalk long enough to nail his big toe, make his shoelaces wave in the breeze. Then I'd blow my horn so she'd come to the window and catch sight of me behind the wheel. Her old fossil of a father would barely be able to stagger up the steps and inside the house, he'd be so scared.

I cruised past my turn. "Hey," Jeff said, "I thought you said once around the block and then you'd put her in the barn."

"I want to swing by a girl's house," I said.

"Why not quit while you're ahead?" he asked me. I didn't answer.

Everything was going without a hitch, better even than I'd thought. I was barreling along at twenty-four miles per when something small and black and furry ran across the street into the path of the car. I turned the wheel sharply. The tires screeched against the pavement. The car got away from me, went up on the sidewalk and slammed into a tree. At the time I would've said it hit a cement bridge, but it turned out to be only a tree. The noise was terrible. The loudest, most terrible noise I'd ever heard. The night reverberated with the sound of splintered glass and grinding metal.

All along the street, doors were flung open, men's voices called, "What in God's name was *that?*" I sat there, my hands still on the wheel, my heart pounding, fighting to get out of my chest.

A man with his napkin still tucked in his belt came running toward me.

"You O.K.?" he called out.

"Sure," I said. "We're O.K." Jeff was leaning against the windshield. I thought he was fooling around. "Jeff," I said, "let's get out of here." He didn't answer. I shook him and his head fell back against the seat. His face wasn't there. Or maybe it was, behind the red pulp that ran down his forehead, dripped off his chin and disappeared inside his sweater.

Maybe Jeff was dead. If he was, I had killed him. What would his mother say? I'd have to tell her. Mrs. Fields, Jeff is dead and I'm responsible.

"Don't move," I told Jeff. It's not good to move a dead man until the doctor sees him. You should never move an accident victim. I opened the door on my side and went around to close the window on Jeff's side so he wouldn't get cold. It was very cold all of a sudden.

"I don't want Jeff to be in a draft," I told the man with his napkin tucked in his belt. "I've got to call the ambulance. Where's Tony? Tony!" I called. "Where are you? Tony's my brother," I told the man.

He caught me as I lurched into him.

"Did you call the ambulance?" he asked someone.

"I told them to get here as fast as they could," a voice answered.

"There's one in the back seat too," another voice said.

"That's Tony," I told them. "He didn't want to come. My father'll kill me if anything happens to Tony."

From a vast distance I heard the siren. After, every time I heard that siren, I wondered who was inside. Then I'd turn my head away the way I did when a funeral procession passed, so people wouldn't think I was trying to see the dead person.

I couldn't see Jeff, I couldn't see Tony. All I could see was the ambulance bearing down on me, its huge yellow eyes picking me out, lighting up the car nestled against the tree, tearing the night apart.

19

"**D**on't look, Charlie. There's blood all over. All over the seat and the ground and everything."

"Why don't they get those kids out of there?"

"The one in front's in bad shape."

Tony was lying on a stretcher. A shadow passed over his face. His eyelids made a tremendous effort to stay up and let in some light. His eyes swam in a sea of nothingness. He sighed and I held his hand.

"It hurts," he whispered.

"How old are you?" a policeman asked me. When I told him, he swore. He wanted my name and my father's and Mr. Fields's name and the registration. He wrote everything down. The flashing light on the ambulance lit up the cardboard faces of the crowd.

An old lady in tennis shoes and a straw hat said,

"Hail Mary, full of grace," several times in a loud voice until someone led her away.

"My father isn't home," I told the policeman who drove me to the hospital in a squad car. "There's no use calling him. He isn't there. Nobody's home. They went to the movies. Nobody will answer."

"Slow down, kid," the policeman said. "We'll take care of it."

We went into the emergency room. I hadn't been there since I broke my arm playing football two years ago.

A crowd of nurses and doctors milled around. Jeff and Tony were somewhere. I couldn't see them.

"This the driver?" a man in a white coat said. I said, "Yes," and he checked me over, made me stand up, walk around, bend my knees, raise my arms.

"You'll do," he said. "Take one of these." He handed me a pill. "Just to relax you. Better sit in the waiting room."

I went in and read an article telling how to build your own log cabin. Someone had cut out the last page so I never did find out how to finish the walls.

Mr. and Mrs. Fields came in. Mrs. Fields sat down and put her arm around me. I wished she'd hit me instead. I could hardly bear the weight of her arm around my shoulders.

"I didn't mean anything," I said. "We were just going to swing around the block once."

She didn't answer. If only she'd holler at me. I'd never seen her so quiet. I wished she'd start chewing me out, telling me how rotten I was, blaming me. Anything. Not just sit there with her arm around me.

Mr. Fields was out in the hall talking to the doctor. He had his hands behind his back. I could see his fingers white and cold looking, lacing, unlacing, holding each other close for comfort.

It was very hot in the waiting room. Mr. Fields beckoned to his wife and she left me and went out into the hall. Presently they disappeared. I was alone.

A guy with his foot wrapped in a dirty bandage sat down next to me.

"Gout," he said, pointing to the bandage. "What's your problem?"

I got up and walked out into the hall. I went to the desk and said, "Can I see Tony Johnson? He's my brother."

The man checked down a list with a pencil. "If you go back and sit down, they'll call you."

I looked into the waiting room. The guy with the bandaged foot was telling another man he wouldn't wish gout on his worst enemy. "It throbs from morning till night," he said. "I'm in agony. If they don't give me something for it tonight, I won't be responsible for what I might do."

It was too hot to stay inside. I went out into the

driveway where the ambulance was parked. My head felt sort of woozy so I sat down on the grass. I wanted to lie down and go to sleep.

A radio was playing. "Now it's time for the nine o'clock news," the announcer said. Nine o'clock. My father and Pat were sitting in the movie, eating popcorn, holding hands. Tony was hurting. Jeff was bleeding. Mr. and Mrs. Fields were standing by Jeff's bed, waiting for him to wake up. If he was going to wake up. I should be standing by Tony's bed so he wouldn't be scared when he opened his eyes and saw all those strangers in white hanging around.

I went back to the desk. "Could I please see Tony Johnson? He's my brother and he's only twelve and my father's at the movies. I have to see him."

The man looked up at me. "You again," he said. "You're the one who wrapped the car around the tree, huh? Little late to start worrying about your brother now, isn't it?" He lifted his lips to show off his stubby brown teeth.

The guy was the kind they get on a child-abuse charge. He'd smack his baby around when it wet its pants or hollered at night. Not to mention if it didn't want to eat its disgusting cereal or something. He didn't have to say that to me. I already knew it. I knew it was too late to worry. He didn't have to tell me. The reason he did was he was a cruel man. He was a sadist. He should be in an institution instead of behind a hospital desk. A sadist was the wrong kind of person to deal with other people who were in need of aid and comfort.

I opened my mouth to tell him what a terrible man he was. I didn't have the strength. I could barely walk. I made it to the men's room and hung over the toilet bowl for a couple of minutes, dry heaving. When I went back to the waiting room, the man with the gout was gone.

20

WHEN I'D ALMOST GIVEN UP, my father and Pat were there.

"Mark," my father said. His face looked bleached. "You're all right?" I nodded. "And Tony? Jeff?"

"They won't tell me anything," I said. "I don't know. I asked a couple of times and they told me to sit here."

My father went to the desk. Pat and I went into the empty waiting room. We sat down, side by side.

"How was the movie?" I asked her.

"Terrible. Are Jeff's parents here?"

"I saw them, then they went away. I've been here for a long time by myself."

"Poor Mark. I'm sorry," Pat said.

Sorry. She doesn't know what sorry is.

She put her hand over mine. I didn't mind. I let it stay. At that moment she was the only friend I

had in the world. That was strange. I must've gone
to sleep. When I woke up, my head was resting on
Pat's shoulder. My neck was stiff.

"What time is it?" I asked.

"Twelve-forty."

"Did Dad come out yet?"

"No," she said.

Much later my father stood in front of us. "You'd
better go home," he said. "I'm going to stay until
Tony comes to. He's in a coma, from shock, they
think."

There were lines in his face that had never been
there before. Deep, dark lines running from his
nose to his mouth. He looked old. My father handed
Pat the car keys. I wanted to throw myself at him,
to put my arms around him and have him do the
same to me. "I'll stay with you, Dad," I said.

He had already turned away. "No," he said. I
didn't want to leave him there alone. He wanted
me to go.

He walked away from us, his shoulders bent,
looking as if it were a difficult job to put one foot in
front of the other. I had done this to him. To Tony
and Jeff. To everybody. Everyone I cared about
was in shreds around me.

We drove home through the dark streets. There
was a light upstairs in the Begoons'. They had a
new baby. I suppose they were feeding it or changing its diapers.

"What if Tony doesn't come out of the coma?" I said in the stillness.

I wanted her to to say, "Of course he'll come out of his coma. Don't be silly."

Instead, she took a long time answering. When she did, all she said was, "All we can do is pray and hope."

I told her about the old lady in sneakers saying, "Hail Mary." I told her about the awful noise the car made when it hit the tree and about the man with the napkin tucked in his belt. "There was this dog, or maybe it was a cat, and it ran in front of the car so I swerved so's not to hit it. That's when it happened."

When we got into the house, she asked me if I wanted some hot milk. If there's anything in this world I really hate, it's hot milk. The smell of it and the scum on top.

"Sure," I said. "That'd be fine."

"It always helps me to sleep," she said, sprinkling cinnamon and nutmeg into the cups. It didn't taste half bad.

We turned out the lights, leaving one on in case Dad came home.

"Thanks for not telling Dad about, you know, that time." I couldn't bring myself to say, "The time I put the moves on you." "I wouldn't have blamed you if you had." She hadn't. I knew that. A lot of people would've.

Pat looked at me. "That's all right," she said.

"And thanks for not giving me a hard time tonight," I said.

She was very tired.

"There's no need," she said. "You're going to be doing that to yourself for a long time to come."

21

FINALLY MY FATHER came home. In late after-noon a taxi pulled up and he got out. Pat ran to meet him. I stayed inside. He paid the driver and they walked up the path together.

"Hi, Dad," I said, opening the door. "How's Tony?"

He lifted his head to look at me. "He came out of the coma, if that's what you want to hear. Fortunately he didn't suffer any brain damage. The doctors say he's going to be all right. He has a couple of cracked ribs so he'll be pretty uncomfortable for a while."

"What about Jeff?" I was afraid to ask. I'd called Mrs. Fields a couple of times during the day but there wasn't any answer.

"Jeff," my father said. "Jeff." He drew his hand across his forehead.

"Why don't you lie down for a bit?" Pat said. I

realized my father probably hadn't slept in more than twenty-four hours.

"In a minute." He patted her cheek. "Jeff will require plastic surgery. His face is badly cut up. I talked to his father this morning. The police said if the car had been going any faster he would've gone through the windshield.

"Jeff is a nice boy. I'm glad for his sake and for yours that that didn't happen."

"Why don't you rest for a while and then talk to Mark?" Pat suggested, trying to ease my father toward the bedroom.

For the first time since they'd been married, she wasn't successful.

Relentlessly my father continued.

"It was almost like a Greek tragedy, your taking that car out on the road," he said. "Inevitable. Something terrible had to happen. You're lucky you got off so easily, Mark. You've been building up to this for more than a year. So much rage inside a person eventually corrodes. I've always thought you've been treated reasonably well."

He lit a cigarette. The smoke snaked around his head. I stood as still as if he'd waved a wand and turned me to stone. That wasn't the way it was, I wanted to say. I wasn't sore. That wasn't why I took the car out for a spin. I was happy. For once, I was happy. I was celebrating a victory over my enemies. That was the way it was.

But what difference would it make if I told him? He wouldn't listen and Tony and Jeff would still be in the hospital and I would still be a shit.

My father went on. "You've been given respect and consideration, and, whether you know it or not, love. I know you're at a bad age. But so am I. So are we all."

He stubbed out the cigarette and with utmost weariness got up.

"I'm going to sleep now, Pat," he said and left the room.

"Thank God they're going to be all right," Pat said. "He's exhausted. It's been very hard for him, Mark."

"If it's O.K. with you," I told her, "I'm going to borrow Tony's bike and cruise around."

"All right. Don't be gone too long."

We were all walking as if we were wading through sand. I got on the bike and aimlessly pedaled through the streets. I parked on a side street and went inside a church and knelt down to pray. It was the only time I'd ever done that without having been made to. I said quite a few prayers and made quite a few promises. One thing I can say about myself is I've never broken a promise. Knowingly, that is.

When it started to get dark, I went home.

"A Mrs. Baumgartner called," Pat said. "She said she'd read about the accident in the paper and she wanted to know if you were all right. I told her you'd call."

"She's one of my customers," I said. I looked up the number, dialed, and waited.

"Yes?" Her voice sounded far away and frail.

"It's Mark, Mrs. Baumgartner. My stepmother told me you called. I'm O.K. We're all O.K."

"Mark," she said. I could hear her smiling. "I'm so glad you called and you're all right. I thought if anything happened to you on top of everything else I didn't know what I'd do."

"How's Henry?" I asked.

"He's going into the home next week. I went to see it yesterday. It's clean and they'll be kind to him. It won't be the same as home, but then, nothing ever is. Mark?"

"Yes?"

"If you'll stop by in the next few days, I want to pay you what I owe you. I kept track of the hours you put in."

"I don't want any money, Mrs. Baumgartner. I told you I was doing the work because I wanted to."

"We'll talk about it when you get here. I'm so glad you're all right. That you all are. So glad."

Me too.

22

"'**D**O YOU KNOW where you are?' they kept asking me," Tony said, relishing each syllable separately. " 'Do you know where you are?' and every time I said, 'Sure. In the hospital.' You know"—his smile cracked his face wide open—"I couldn't help feeling that they were disappointed that I had the right answer. I think they wanted me to say, 'No, where am I?' But I fooled 'em."

Tony was definitely out of his coma.

"The nurse told me that's what they always ask a patient who's coming out of a coma," Tony informed us importantly. "They want to make sure the patient has all his marbles, that his brain's in one piece."

A nurse's aide came into the room smiling, smelling of flowers and rubbing alcohol. She handed Tony a glass of orange juice.

"Anything else I can get you?" she asked.

"How about a steak and some French fries?" Tony said.

"Dream on, lover," she replied and glided out on her rubber-soled shoes.

"If we don't get him out of here soon, he's going to be spoiled rotten," Pat said.

"Can I come home today?" Tony asked.

My father touched him on the forehead lightly.

"Not today," he said. "Maybe tomorrow. They want to keep an eye on you. Make sure you don't leap up and start doing push-ups or high hurdles. The ribs will mend faster if you stay quiet."

"Listen, Dad, I'm not messing around with those ribs," Tony said. "Every time I move they let me know they're there."

"Hello, Doctor," my father said to a man who paused at the door. "I was hoping you'd come while we were here. Pat, this is Dr. Barnes. My wife and son Mark, Doctor."

"How do you do?" Dr. Barnes was tall and thin with ruddy cheeks and a bald head. He looked the way a doctor should look: wise and strong. And competent.

"Thought I'd stop by to see how the young man was doing. Got any complaints, Tony?" the doctor asked.

"Nope. Only that I'd like to go home," Tony said.

"In good time. All in good time." He turned to

me. "You managed to survive without any side effects?" he said. I kept my face carefully blank. I guess he knew all about me. I wasn't used to people knowing about me. I nodded and wished he'd stop looking at me with that expression on his face.

"If you're going to hang around for a while," I said to Pat and my father, "I think I'll check and see if they'll let me see Jeff for a couple of minutes."

"All right." They let me go without a struggle. I could hear them all laughing as I trudged down the hall.

The nurse told me I could see Jeff if I stayed for five minutes. No more. Five minutes would do it. Maybe he wouldn't speak to me. Maybe he'd tell me to get out, that our friendship was over, that his mother and father didn't want him to associate with me ever again.

I knocked on his door and opened it a crack.

"Hey," I said, "it's me. I came to see how you were."

"Hey, turkey." Jeff's voice came out in a croak. "Am I glad to see you. How do you like me?"

Most of his face was swathed in bandages. The eyes peered out on the world as sparkly and bright as ever. I concentrated on his eyes.

"How are things?" I asked him. A stupid question, everything considered. "How do you feel?"

"You ought to stick around and catch the night

nurse," Jeff said. "She's some classy broad. She comes in here, pussyfoots over to my bed, puts her cool hand on my fevered brow, and says in this soft voice, 'Is there anything you'd like? Anything I can do for you?' "

Jeff shifted in the bed. "Man, she doesn't know it, but those are leading questions. If I wasn't all taped up, I could give her a run for her money."

We smiled at each other. The night nurse was probably a grandmother about ten times and her feet hurt and she had varicose veins.

"Maybe I'll come back tonight when she's here," I told him. "She sounds like somebody I could get interested in."

"Definitely. Very definitely."

"They told me I could only stay five minutes," I said, fast. "I just wanted to check and make sure you were all right. I was going to tell you I was sorry but I figured that might be dumb. You know that anyway."

"Sorry for what? You're the one's going to be sorry. Those docs are going to stitch me up into such a handsome dude the girls will drop like flies in a huge circle around me. All you're going to get is my rejects."

The door opened and the nurse looked in. "I'm sorry," she said, "but it's time for visitors to leave."

She stood there. Obviously she wasn't going to go until I did. I went over to the bed and took Jeff's hand.

"Well," I said, "I might as well be going. Just wanted to see how you were doing."

We shook hands.

"When you come again, I want you to bring me some of those magazines with naked girls on the cover," he said in a voice that carried a couple of miles. "Don't forget."

"I won't," I promised. There wasn't anything else to say.

"I'm glad you came, Mark," he said.

"Sure," I answered.

When I got back to Tony's room, they were still laughing.

23

THAT NIGHT I HAD the dream for the first time. I was driving along a slippery road. A tunnel loomed ahead and a sign said, "Remove sunglasses before entering tunnel." I didn't have on any sunglasses but still the tunnel was dark, with slick, sloping sides, like a toboggan run. I drove faster to get out into the sunlight I could see ahead. Just as I thought I had it made, a steel door slammed down in front of me, like in a James Bond movie. I put my foot on the brakes as hard as I could, but it didn't do any good. My car hit the steel door with such impact that the door and the car, with me in it, melted in flames and hideous sounds.

"I didn't mean to," I said, sitting up in bed. "Please, it's not my fault. I didn't mean to."

My father stood by the side of my bed, silhouetted against the light from the hall.

"Didn't mean to what, Mark?" he said.

"It's O.K.," I mumbled. "It was just a dream."

"Would you like a glass of water?" he asked me.

"No thanks," I said. "I'm sorry I bothered you."

Pat came in behind him. "Maybe a glass of hot milk would help," she said.

"He's all right," my father said. He took her by the arm and turned her toward the door. "He's perfectly all right."

"Why don't you let him say how he is?" she asked in a tight voice. "Would you like some hot milk, Mark?"

"No thanks," I said again. "I'm practically asleep now." I pulled up the covers high around my ears and shut my eyes. The trouble with that was, pictures snuck up behind my eyelids; pictures of Tony and Jeff stretched out, side by side, on a marble slab, and where their eyes were supposed to be, there were tiny dark caverns, empty caverns, staring up at me.

"Maybe he ought to see a psychiatrist," I heard Pat say. Their bedroom door must be open a crack. "Maybe a good one could help Mark."

"No," my father said. His voice rose and he sounded angry. I had never heard him use that tone of voice to her before.

There was a silence. I opened my eyes so I could listen better.

"Why are you so against psychiatry? I went to see a good doctor when I was going through my divorce and he helped me a great deal. Why have you closed your mind against something that might help him?"

"The kid is going to have to work this out for himself." My father's voice was cold and positive. "He doesn't need some expensive assistance to make him see how selfish he was. He's fourteen years old. If I'd taken the family car at that age and wrapped it around a tree, either with or without my brother and a friend in it, my father would've handled it without benefit of psychiatry. It's too easy to resort to that. For some things, yes. For out-and-out self-centeredness, no."

Another silence. "Then I'm glad I never knew your father," Pat said. "What applied when you were a boy doesn't necessarily apply to Mark."

"The basic concepts of right and wrong remain unchanged." I knew how my father's face must look as he said this: thin and unyielding.

"I never knew you stood in judgment on people," Pat said slowly. "I thought your mind was open, not closed. Open to all sorts of things. I thought you were a kind, loving man. A compassionate man. I can see I was wrong."

I heard her go down the hall, down the stairs. My father shut the door firmly. That was all.

Dad and Pat were fighting. They were having a fight over me. The first chink in the armor, the first ravel in the sleeve. All over me. At one time, like a couple of days ago, I would've felt triumphant. As it was, I felt like a bastard. A lousy, big-nosed bastard.

I turned over on my stomach and tried to burrow deep into the mattress and go back to sleep. Me go to a psychiatrist? All the guy does is listen to you. Why not? He gets plenty of bread to listen. Like about fifty bucks an hour. I don't think I could talk about myself for an hour straight. On the other hand, if I was paying the guy that kind of scratch, I could make up a few things—dreams and stuff. They're big on dreams. That and how you feel about your parents. Do you hate them, tolerate them, or wish they'd get lost? Not to mention your siblings. Do you have a subconscious desire to rub out your little brother? Is that why you wrapped the car around a tree with him in it? Hell, I could be my own psychiatrist and cut down on expenses.

I've got to pull myself together. I'm going to be in hock for a long time. After I finish paying for the damage on the new car, I have to start paying Mr. Fields for the plastic surgeon. Jeff says he can't decide if he wants the doc to make him look like Robert Redford or Rudolph Valentino. Rudolph Valentino was this really cool Latin cat who had the dames flopping in the aisles like a mess of beached trout.

Plastic surgeons are very expensive, I understand. I'm going to have to work my butt off for the next ten years. Maybe longer.

I went to see Mrs. Baumgartner this afternoon.

A tall, thin man was sitting in the kitchen drinking a can of beer.

"This is my son, Joe, Mark," she said. Joe said "Hi" to me without really acknowledging my presence.

"Mark's been a tremendous help to us the past few months," Mrs. Baumgartner told Joe. "I don't know what we'd have done without him."

"Is that right?" Joe said. "I notice a big change in Dad since I was last here," he said to his mother. "He's going downhill fast."

"He might hear you, Joe He's in the next room. He understands everything you say." Her cheeks were flushed and her hands trembled.

"Mom," Joe said in a patient tone, raising his eyebrows, "you're kidding yourself. He's a vegetable."

"No, he's not." My voice sounded very loud, even to me. Joe sat up and looked at me for the first time. "He knows me whenever I come. He listens to conversations. He listens when he's read to."

Mrs. Baumgartner smiled at me. "You're absolutely right, Mark." I knew she was pleased by what I'd said.

Joe got up and put on his jacket. "O.K., then, tell him I said good-bye. Let me know when you take him to the home and I'll come see him." He leaned over to kiss his mother and she stood, rigid, while he bussed her on the cheek. "So long, kid," Joe said and was gone.

"Well," she said. "Well. There you have it. That's my son." I didn't say anything because I couldn't think of anything to say.

"It's a terrible thing to dislike your own child," Mrs. Baumgartner said.

A thought came into my head that I would just as soon hadn't; I wondered if my father felt that way about me. I felt depressed when I realized it was a possibility.

"Henry's having a nap, otherwise I'd say go and talk to him," she said. "He tires very easily. After, after, he . . . goes, I'll go into an apartment. It won't be too bad. You'll come to see me?"

"Whenever you want," I told her.

"You know what you said about it taking a lot of energy just to stay alive?" I asked her. "And how it was worth it? The older I get, the more I know you're right."

"I'm glad you decided that," she said. "You'll make a good man. I'm sure of that."

"I don't think my father will ever forgive me."

"Yes, he will," she said. "It may be tough going, but he will."

I wish I could be as convinced as Mrs. Baumgartner. That everything will turn out all right.

Do you know where you are?

The words keep coming at me. No answer.

If I did answer, it might be different today from tomorrow. So. No answer at all.

CONSTANCE C. GREENE has been writing for many years, starting in Manhattan as a reporter for the Associated Press. In 1969 she began her career as a children's book author and has since written many books for Viking, including *A Girl Called Al* and *Beat the Turtle Drum,* both ALA Notable Books. She is one of the leading writers of contemporary fiction for young people.

Mrs. Greene and her husband live on Long Island. They have five children, all now grown.

F   Greene, Constance C.
GREENE
     Getting nowhere

S22217

DATE			